BURY THE HATCHET

George Carter and his family lived peacefully in the small town of Uphill. But one fateful weekend something caused them to experience real fear and act completely out of character. The first trigger was when they learned that a homicidal maniac was at large in Uphill, carrying a damaged suitcase containing his victim's body parts. The second trigger was on finding that their new lodger's suitcase was also damaged — and the grisly truth of what was inside . . .

JOHN RUSSELL FEARN
Edited by Philip Harbottle

◆

BURY THE HATCHET

Complete and Unabridged

LINFORD
Leicester

First published in Great Britain

First Linford Edition
published 2011

The moral right of the author
has been asserted

British Library CIP Data

Fearn, John Russell, *1908 – 1960.*
  Bury the hatchet.- -
  (Linford mystery library)
  1. Murderers- -Fiction.
  2. Suspense fiction.
  3. Large type books.
  I. Title II. Series
  823.9′12–dc22

  ISBN 978–1–4448–0897–1

Published by
F. A. Thorpe (Publishing)
Anstey, Leicestershire

Set by Words & Graphics Ltd.
Anstey, Leicestershire
Printed and bound in Great Britain by
T. J. International Ltd., Padstow, Cornwall

This book is printed on acid-free paper

1

It was 6.45 on a November evening in 1957. Mrs. Ruth Carter was in her living room, putting the finishing touches to an almost laid table for four. The room was in a state of 'orderly untidiness'. On the settee lay the comic strip section from a newspaper, and the cheerful room typified those used by thousands of families throughout Britain. There was a large table, a sideboard on which stood a radio; and doors that led to hall and kitchen. There was a coal fire burning and curtains drawn across the window. On the back of the hall door reposed a coat hanger.

In the midst of her table preparations, humming a tune to herself, Mrs. Carter turned at the sound of her husband George entering by the hall door. He was a quiet businesslike type, wearing a soft hat and overcoat, and carrying an evening paper. Ridding himself of his hat and coat, he hung up his suit jacket behind the door and struggled into a pullover.

'Everything all right, dear?' Ruth enquired.

'Oh, not so bad,' her husband sighed, 'Looks as though I'm first home for a change.' He crossed to his favourite armchair and seated himself, opening his evening paper.

Mrs. Carter hovered busily in the kitchen doorway. 'Seems so . . . But it doesn't matter. We can start without the girls. You know what they are! Being Friday night and wages in their handbags they might go anywhere. Anywhere!'

George frowned, then said vaguely, 'Seems silly to me. When you get paid you expect to come home and — '

'Not at seventeen and nineteen you don't! I know I didn't. Come on, dear — get on with your meal.'

George crossed to the table and sat down rather gloomily, leaving his paper in the armchair. Ruth started to pour tea, then hesitated as she noted his expression.

'Is there something the matter, George?'

'Yes, plenty! To cut a long story short I didn't get that promotion I was hoping for, or the raise that would have gone with it. I'm still head salesman and not the production manager, as I'd hoped.'

Ruth resumed pouring the tea. 'That's too bad, dear . . . Here, have a drink.'

George took the filled cup. 'I'm just as I was. Me! A man of my talent. It's downright disgusting. Look, Ruth, do you realize — '

His wife smiled faintly. 'Yes, dear, I do. With your knowledge of chemistry and crime you ought to have been a backroom specialist helping Scotland Yard. Your test for bloodstains is the most efficient in history . . . ' She bustled off to the kitchen and returned with a plateful of food. 'Irish stew, dear. I know you love it.'

'Thanks.' George grasped his wife's hand. 'I'm sorry, dear. I really thought promotion was in the bag. Makes me look a shocking failure.'

'Oh, get away with you.' Ruth sat down to her own meal. 'As a matter of fact I never thought you'd get it. Not this year, anyway.'

'Oh, you didn't! Then why on earth did you let us get that washing machine on the never-never? We only risked it on the strength of my getting that raise. We could have waited. I don't know how we're going to meet it.'

Ruth smiled complacently. 'But I do. I was prepared for this. The whole thing's taken care of in the newsagent's window.'

'Newsagent's window? What are you talking about?'

'An advertisement, George . . . Like the stew?'

'Yes, dear, lovely. But what's this about an advertisement?'

'Simple enough. Er — you have an upstairs room specially for chemistry experiments, photography, and whatnot, haven't you?'

'Well?' George's voice held an ominous note.

'Well you haven't any more.' Ruth gave a casual shrug. 'I've put all your bottles and things in the wash-house, and Laboratory Number One is now a double bedroom, available for renting.'

'Is it now? And when did all this transformation take place?'

'Oh, it's been going on for days! Trudy

has a rough idea what's coming, but you haven't. You haven't experimented for some time, so that gave me the opportunity to clear things out. I'm going to offer board-residence or bed and breakfast. The money will make up the extra you would have got, and by the end of the year you'll surely have got promotion . . . ' She paused, thinking. 'If our prospective lodger should be a fat man it won't matter, being a double bed.'

'How do you know it will be a man?' George asked, archly. 'It might be a very attractive young woman.'

'George!'

'Sorry. It *is* possible, though.'

'If that happens I'll take care of it . . . Now, I've got a double bed rolled up behind the pantry door, and the old one is dropped in a corner of the kitchen ready for — ' she broke off as Trudy, their eldest daughter, came in from the hall doorway. Clad in outdoor clothes, she tripped over the mat at the inside of the door.

'So help me,' Trudy muttered to herself, 'I'll fix that thing yet.' She tugged off her hat and coat and threw them carelessly aside. 'How's everybody? What's to eat, mum?'

Ruth got to her feet. 'Irish stew.'

'God bless the Irish.' Trudy switched on the radio on the sideboard, and came across to the table. 'Well, anything happened?'

'Why should it?' her father asked dryly. 'What did you expect — royalty?'

'I'm only trying to be sociable, dad,' Trudy pouted.

Her mother got up to go back into the kitchen. 'No, nothing's happened. Nothing ever does that's worthwhile reporting.'

George glanced at Trudy. 'You're late, aren't you?'

'Yes,' the girl admitted, 'but I didn't do it on purpose — not with an appetite like mine. We had overtime to do, and being Friday we just had to finish it.'

'You'll be paid for it, of course?'

Trudy sighed. 'Not as far as I know. Only a few minutes extra.'

George frowned. 'And those few minutes tot up to a sizeable amount by the end of a year. Capitalists! That's what

6

they are. I've a good mind to tell them that my eldest daughter is a stenographer and not a slave. Huh! Who do they think they are?'

'My bread and butter. And they'd be quick to say so!'

Ruth came back in with the stew for Trudy, then paused to listen to the radio announcer.

' . . . There is still no solution regarding the Uphill murder, although Scotland Yard is working on several lines of inquiry. It will be remembered that Christine Ashton, aged 17, was the victim of a brutal hatchet murder recently.'

The bulletin continued as the three at the table tackled their meal.

'From traces found so far, the police believe the killer is carrying the dismembered head and legs of his victim around with him in a suitcase with a broken handle. The public is warned that this maniac is dangerous. As near as can be estimated he is nearly six feet tall, dark haired and blue eyed, with a deceptively pleasing manner. His conversation is queer at times, but otherwise may be regarded as normal. Anybody winking at him may cause him to lose control. The same effect is produced by uttering the word 'Asparagus'.

'Anybody seeing or encountering such a person should call Whitehall 1212, or any police station.'

Trudy looked up, smiling broadly. 'Lovely, isn't it? I love murders — especially the juicy ones!'

'Trudy, how *can* you!' Ruth protested. 'It's put me right off my meal.'

'From the north of England,' the radio announcement continued, 'there is still no further news of Arthur Smart, the young man who astonished theatrical circles recently with — '

George got up suddenly and switched off the radio. 'That's enough of that! Chopping up bodies. It's especially horrible when we happen to live in Uphill ourselves. It must be over a week since that girl was murdered on the waste land back of Forsythe's chip shop. Time something was done!'

He resumed his seat at table.

Trudy ate heartily. 'Well, I didn't see

8

any man about six feet and carrying a suitcase with a broken handle, otherwise I'd have been home a lot quicker! Incidentally, where's Fay? Oughtn't she to be in?'

'She ought to be, yes, but there's no sign of her.' Ruth looked worried. 'George, I don't want to say it, but do you think — '

'No, I don't,' George said firmly. 'Now don't start worrying or you'll get one of your attacks of nerves.'

'By the way, when do we get the telly back?' Trudy asked plaintively. 'Seems ages since the engineer took it away for repair.'

George glanced at her. 'He says the tube's gone, and it's going to cost something like a week's wages to put things right. Of course, that won't matter much if a certain bright idea of your mother's comes off.'

'*What* bright idea?' Trudy asked. 'What's been going on, mum?'

'Well, as a matter of fact — '

Ruth broke off as there came the unmistakable sounds of Fay, their younger daughter

coming into the house — and also stum-
bling over the mat.

'Oh, bother it! If I felt energetic I'd fix
that thing!' She laid her coat carefully
on the hanger behind the door, before
entering the dining room.

'Hello, chain gang! Sorry I'm late.'

'We're not,' Trudy remarked.

'Oh come now, Trudy,' her father
admonished, 'is that any way to greet
your sister?'

'Course it is,' Trudy said blandly. 'Can't
think of a better.' She eyed Fay sitting
dreamily at the table, and added: 'As a
matter of interest, Fay Carter, where have
you been until this time?'

Fay looked up. 'Does it matter?'

'Not really.' Trudy shrugged. 'Can't
blame a girl for trying.'

Once again Ruth Carter went into the
kitchen in search of more stew.

'I haven't been anywhere, really,' Fay
said, as Trudy continued to look at her.
'At least not anywhere in particular. I've
been hunting for an 'Evening in Paradise'.

'You're not likely to find it in Uphill,'
her father remarked dryly.

10

'So I've discovered.' Fay sighed as her mother placed the stew before her. 'Thanks, mum . . . Oh, I *did* so want to hear Lanny Bilgraves' latest song.'

'Lanny Bilgrave?' George raised an eyebrow. 'What's he got to do with an evening in Paradise?'

Fay looked her surprise. 'Why, everything! He sings it!'

'Lanny Bilgrave is a pop singer, George,' Ruth pointed out patiently.

Her husband gave an expression of mock disgust: 'Oh, another of those groaners. Perhaps it's as well you didn't find the record. We've enough hardships without listening to those dirging Romeos.'

'All right!' Fay snapped. 'No need to pitch into me just because I like Lanny Bilgrave.'

'Not only Lanny Bilgrave, either,' Trudy remarked. 'You'd like anything with trousers on.'

'Now look here, Trudy — '

'Oh, stop it, you two,' Ruth Carter admonished. 'Get on with your meal.'

Trudy gave her a glance. 'Mum, you were saying something about something

11

when Curly Locks here burst in on us.'

'Something about something?' her mother looked vague.

George finished his meal, rose, and headed to his armchair to read the newspaper: 'You know! About my work-room.'

'About dad's workroom?' Trudy frowned. 'But what's that got to do with getting the telly tube repaired? That's what *I* was talking about.'

George picked up his paper and settled into his seat. 'According to your mother my workroom solves the problem.'

Fay looked surprised. 'Great Scot, you don't mean a — lodger?'

'I certainly do,' Ruth said flatly. 'Any objections?'

'None at all.' Fay beamed. 'Might be a nice young man!'

Trudy pushed her cleared plate aside. 'Good Lord, don't you *ever* think of anything else but males?'

'Yes.' George Carter peeped around his newspaper. 'Pop singers.'

'All right, all right.' Fay sighed heavily. 'I'm not the only one with faults.' She

12

rose from the table. 'Thanks, mum, that was smashing. I wish I had time to eat it all but I've got to dash!'

As she headed for the hall door, she spoke over her shoulder: 'I've got to meet Dick at 7:30.'

George lowered his paper. 'You're not going out *again*?'

'Of course. No sense in stopping in, especially when there's no telly.'

'Doesn't it occur to you that there might be something more important to do than entertaining yourself? How about giving your mother a hand for a change?'

'Oh, Trudy will do that. She always does . . . ' She glanced at her sister, who was quietly helping their mother to clear the table. Fay made to leave, then hesitated as her father raised a hand.

'Fay, come here for a moment. I want to speak to you.'

Fay sighed heavily. 'Well, what's wrong? And do hurry up, dad. I'm late as it is.'

'You're not going until you hear what I have to say . . . First, you're a very attractive young woman — '

'I know that. Dick's told me as much.'

George frowned. 'Candidly, Fay, I'd much rather you didn't go out tonight — at least not alone.'

'But I can't meet Dick with an escort, now can I? He'd think I'd gone off him.'

'I'll make it plainer. If Dick is the kind of chap I think he is, have him come here to fetch you in future, and also bring you home. He must never leave your side — at least for the time being.'

'But he lives right on the other side of town!' Fay protested. 'We've an arrangement to meet in the town centre. He just couldn't come all this way.' She gave her father a puzzled look. 'You're not making sense, dad.'

'I'm trying to tell you that we're living in Uphill, where quite recently a youngster of about your age was brutally murdered by a maniac with a hatchet — '

'What's that got to do with meeting Dick?'

'Just this,' George tightened his lips. 'The maniac is still at large, according to the radio tonight, and he's probably in Uphill, too. He's carrying a suitcase with a broken handle and . . . and it has the remains of his latest victim inside it. The girl's name was Christine Ashton. What happened to her could happen to you!'

Fay shrugged carelessly. 'I'll risk it. Every girl in Uphill can't sit by the fireside just because this nut is running about ... ' The girl crossed to the hall door, then looked back. 'Don't worry about me. I know how to look after myself!'

She swept out, headed for her room to get ready to go out on her date.

George shook his head. 'Oh, I give up! What's the use?'

At that moment Trudy came back from the kitchen. 'Use of what, dad?'

'It's nothing — I hope. Just Fay acting up again, that's all.'

Trudy picked up the condiment stand from the table. 'I heard you saying something about Christine Ashton? Were you warning Fay about the maniac?'

'Yes. I only hope she doesn't have to learn by experience!'

Ruth's voice came from the kitchen. 'Trudy, come and wipe, will you?'

'Coming, mum ... ' Trudy dumped

the condiments on the sideboard and returned to the kitchen.

George read his paper for a short while, then got up and took his football coupon from the mantlepiece. Clearing a space on the table, he settled down at it with his coupon and permutation guide.

He gave a start as there came the sound of a dish dropped in the kitchen. Then Trudy swept in, and with a good deal of clatter, began putting the crockery out of the way.

George tightened his lips as his wife came in with a carpet sweeper, causing him to turn into an acrobat to get his feet out of the way.

Trudy had been surveying the troublesome mat by the door. Abruptly she made up her mind. She went into the kitchen, to emerge with a hammer and some tacks, and proceeded to tack down the mat violently.

George threw up his hands. 'Trudy, do you mind?'

'What?' Trudy continued to bang the hammer vigorously. 'Mind what?'

'I'm trying to do my coupon. Can't I

have a bit of peace? It'd be quieter in the main street!'

Trudy straightened up. 'Sorry. The mat will do now, I think.'

'I should hope so!' her father commented sourly. 'From the noise you were making I was half expecting the floorboards to go through.' As Trudy took the hammer back to the kitchen, he returned thankfully to his coupon.

His respite was short lived, for after a moment Trudy returned, this time with a vacuum cleaner. Plugging in, she commenced to clean under the table, causing more acrobatics by her exasperated father.

'Sorry!' Trudy apologized. 'But mum says you shouldn't make so many crumbs. The sweeper just isn't good enough.'

The vacuuming continued as George struggled to complete his coupon. Finally, responding to frantic signals, Trudy switched off. 'Mum's orders, dad . . . '

She dragged the vacuum back to the kitchen.

George settled again to his coupon, watching warily as Ruth came back in.

17

She commenced to sort out newspapers with a good deal of crackling noise.

Trudy came back and sprawled herself on the settee, picking up the comic strip supplement, and settling to read it. Every now and again, she abstractedly snapped the lid of her reading glasses case. At about the fourth 'snap' George could stand it no longer, and jumped up.

'Quiet, the pair of you! Please!'

Ruth glanced at him amusedly. 'Coupon, I suppose? I'd forgotten that even the mice have to wear plimsolls at this vital moment . . . What are you aiming for, George? Seventy five thousand?'

'I'm aiming for the best I can get, if only I can get a bit of peace!'

'Yes, dear. Sorry. I wouldn't deprive you of £75,000 for anything.' She sat down and picked up some sewing.

George silently congratulated himself on the return of peace, and settled down again to his coupon. After a moment or two, he started violently as rock and roll music suddenly burst forth from Fay's bedroom.

He leapt up and strode to the hall door.

18

'I give up!' He wrenched the door open. 'Fay! Fay! Turn off that confounded row!'

The music stopped abruptly, and George returned to his coupon. After a moment or two Fay appeared, dressed for an evening out.

George glared at her. 'What the dickens do you mean by it? Making that din with that damned jungle music!'

Trudy looked up from reading the comic strip supplement. 'Don't look now, dad, but you're a square.'

'A square?' George looked his puzzlement.

'Trudy's right dad. If you've no appreciation of the pops you're definitely a square. You're just not in the groove.'

'Groove?' George asked hazily.

'No,' Fay asserted. 'You're a square all right, and that's the lowest form of animal life. You're not cool.'

'You can bet your life I'm not.' George was nettled. 'And if you call me the lowest form of animal life again I'll use a hairbrush to you, even if you are seventeen!'

Fay sighed heavily. 'Gosh, dad, but you're

old fashioned. Just because I play some pop music to get me in the mood for the evening you have to raise the roof — '

'I rather thought it was you who was doing that!' George said heavily. 'It's beyond my understanding why a girl should have to play records to get herself in the mood. I certainly didn't need that kind of stimulus when your mother and I were walking out together.'

'That was different,' Fay derided. 'I don't suppose you ever went jiving. That's what I mean by getting in the mood. The rest comes naturally.' She glanced at her watch. 'Anyway, I've got to be going.'

Her mother looked up from her sewing. 'And don't be late!'

'And be careful.' Her father added. 'Remember what I told you.'

Fay laughed. 'I will. Be back about quarter to twelve, I expect.' She went out, and George sighed at the inevitable slamming of the front door.

He put his completed coupon in an envelope. 'I'm a bit late with the coupon this week, but I'll risk the midnight mail. Shan't be long.' He crossed to the hall, then after a moment reappeared in hat and coat. 'By the way, is that a comic strip you're reading, Trudy?'

'Sure is.'

'Don't forget to save *Superman* for me before your mother yanks it off for firelights. I want to find out where he took the Empire State Building to . . . '

2

After George had left, Ruth looked fondly at her eldest daughter, 'Why don't you ever find a boy, Trudy?'

'Who? Me?' Trudy looked up. 'Not likely! Not when I've got a good home to stop in. Besides, I work hard enough at the office without spending my spare time chasing round with pimply teddy boys.'

'But they're not *all* teddy boys, dear.'

'They are as far as I'm concerned.' Trudy yawned, stretching. 'Besides, I'm a career woman.'

'Of course, love.' Ruth smiled faintly. 'I'd forgotten.'

'Besides, I don't feel like going out — not with a maniac running around. Never know what might happen . . . ' Trudy frowned. 'I do wish Fay would have a bit sense! I'm rather surprised you aren't more worried, mum.'

'I am really,' Ruth sighed, 'but I try to take consolation from the thought that

Providence watches over children and drunken men.'

'But Fay *isn't* a child!'

Rising, Ruth put aside her sewing. 'That's what *you* think, Trudy. Frankly, there are times when I wonder if she will ever grow up . . . However, enough of this! I've things to do. I promised to call in and have a few words with Mrs. Engleton this evening. You don't mind?'

'Why, no!' Trudy's voice held a slightly hollow note. 'Why should I?'

'I was thinking of the maniac being about.'

'Oh, that's outside. I'm safe enough in the house. In any case, dad won't be long . . . '

Thus reassured, Ruth went to get her hat and coat from the hall, before returning the doorway. 'I shan't be any longer than I can help, dear. As you know, Mrs. Engleton is a bit of a natterer, so if I'm not back by half past eight put a light under the kettle . . . 'bye, love.'

'You're not afraid of the maniac, then? You'll have quite a few badly lighted streets to cross.'

Ruth smiled. 'As Fay herself said: 'Everybody in Uphill can't sit by the fireside just because a nut with a hatchet is running about . . . ' So I'll risk it.' She kissed Trudy and went out.

Trudy continued to read for a while, then her nerves got the better of her. She got up from the settee and wandered about for a while, doing needless little tasks.

She started as the front door bell rang. As she hesitated, the ring was repeated. Reluctantly, she went through the hall doorway, and opened the door.

She was considerably surprised to find a young couple.

The woman was a fashionably dressed blonde and a decidedly cheerful-looking young man with dark hair. Trudy judged there were both in their late twenties.

'We've come about the room,' the man said. 'Mr. and Mrs. Bradbury.'

'Oh . . . You saw the advertisement in the newsagent's window, then?'

'Yes,' the woman smiled. 'And so we thought we'd pop along and get all the details.'

'Yes, of course . . . ' Trudy's confidence began to return. 'Well then, you'd better come in.'

Inside, Trudy indicated the settee. 'Sit down, won't you?' As the couple settled, she added: 'I'm afraid I can't tell you very much. Mother's just gone out and dad's out too.'

The young man smiled pleasantly. 'Then you're . . . all alone?'

'Yes; I'm afraid I am,' Trudy agreed uncomfortably. 'You couldn't come back, I suppose?'

The blonde pondered. 'Perhaps we'd better.'

At that moment the front door banged. As the three looked expectantly towards the hall doorway, Fay entered, looking very disconsolate.

'Oh, it's you!' Trudy exclaimed, surprised. She glanced at the visitors. 'My younger sister, Fay . . . Fay, this is Mr. and Mrs. Bradbury. They've come about the room mother's advertising.'

Fay hesitated momentarily, then shook hands, smiling. 'Glad to know you . . . Don't expect any sense out of Trudy.

Mother's got everything in hand . . . Excuse me a moment, will you?'

She hurried out.

Bradbury glanced at Trudy. 'Your sister seems a very nice girl.'

'Fay?' Trudy shrugged. 'Oh, she's all right. A bit wild, maybe.'

Mrs. Bradbury looked at her husband. 'Well, Jim, it seems that we'd better come back later — ' She broke off as Fay re-entered, having taken off her outdoor clothes.

Fay moodily sought out a chair and sat down. Trudy gave her a quick glance.

'What happened to bring you home again?'

Fay looked up. 'Dick has to work overtime,' she explained glumly. 'He sent his kid brother to tell me.'

'Oh well, never mind,' Bradbury remarked cheerfully. 'Don't feel too cut up about it.'

'Please don't *say* that!' Trudy cried, with a little shudder.

Jim Bradbury seemed surprised at her sharp reaction. 'Why not? I'm sorry but — What was wrong with what I said?

'About being cut up, I mean,' Trudy explained. 'Maybe you don't know there's a maniac loose in Uphill?'

'Is there really?' Immediately Bradbury became sympathetic. 'Oh, I see! You've got nerves. Well, I suppose that's not to be wondered at.'

There came the sound of a key in the lock and the bumping of the front door as George Carter returned. On entering, he pulled off his hat and coat.

'Oh, hello!' he exclaimed, on seeing the visitors. 'Good evening! What goes on?'

'Mr. and Mrs. Bradbury — my father,' Trudy hastily made the introductions. As he shook hands, Trudy added: 'They're interested in the room mother's advertising.'

'Oh, I see. Splendid . . . As far as I'm concerned you are both welcome but I can't do anything much until my wife returns. She has everything in hand — ' George broke off as he became aware of Fay. 'I thought you'd gone to jive?'

'Dick couldn't come,' Fay explained briefly. 'Overtime.'

'I could go and fetch mother, dad,'

27

Trudy suggested, as the visitors hovered uncertainly. 'And then Mr. and Mrs. Bradbury wouldn't have the trouble of coming again.'

'You could,' her father said, 'but I'd much rather you didn't. The streets aren't safe for any girl with a hatchet murderer running loose. Probably your mother won't be long, anyway.' He turned to his visitors. 'I could show you the room, and by that time my wife Ruth might have got back.' As Bradbury smiled and nodded, he went on. 'Okay, come this way.'

They followed him through the hall doorway.

Fay turned to her sister. 'They don't seem so bad — him especially. Did you notice what nice blue eyes and dark hair he's got?'

Trudy frowned. 'Dark hair? Blue eyes?' She gave herself a little shake. 'About six feet and a deceptively pleasing manner . . . Oh, *Lord*!'

'*Now* what's the matter with you?' Fay demanded.

'N-nothing,' Trudy stammered. 'You didn't hear the radio announcement about the Uphill maniac, did you?'

'No.' Fay shrugged. 'Doesn't matter, does it?'

'But it does!' Trudy insisted. 'This fellow Bradbury has all the qualifications!' She paused, taking a grip on herself. 'It must be coincidence — but watch out if he talks a little queer. The radio warned us about that, but it didn't say anything about a glamorous blonde.'

'That's the main thing, as a rule — Oh, stop being a drip, Trudy! Mr. What's-His-Name is no more a maniac than I am. Why, he's perfectly delightful and smiles all the time.'

Trudy remained unconvinced. 'Yes, I know — deceptively genial . . . Her manner changed as she added tartly: 'Of course you *would* have to find him perfect, just because he's a man. Oh well, I suppose I'm behaving like an idiot.'

At length George Carter and Mr. and Mrs. Bradbury returned, deep in conversation.

' . . . and there it is,' George was saying. 'It's only a matter of fixing things with the wife now.'

'Just the thing we've been looking for,' Bradbury smiled. 'We've been all round the district, then quite by chance we saw your advertisement in the newsagent's window. Must be our lucky night.' He and his wife resumed their seats on the settee. 'You see,' Bradbury went on, 'Vera and I want a sort of temporary shakedown'.

'To be near your work, I presume?' George asked.

'Not particularly,' Vera Bradbury remarked. 'We're on holiday at present.'

Fay smiled cynically. 'In a dump like Uphill? Well, you're certainly not choosy.'

Bradbury glanced at her, unruffled. 'Oh, Uphill isn't so bad. I've been in worse places. What I like is the open country around it — the peace — where one can be quiet. One is never afraid of being watched . . . The quiet does something to me.'

'You sort of want to be alone?' Fay suggested.

'At times — and my wife quite understands.'

'I suppose you like the quiet so that you

can think?' Trudy asked.

'Yes . . . ' Bradbury agreed. 'Lots of men and women too — do a lot of thinking. From such little acorns big oaks do grow.'

His odd remark caused Fay and Trudy to exchange significant looks.

'Anything in particular you think about?' Fay asked lightly.

'Oh, yes!' Bradbury responded cheerfully. 'Chiefly knives, cabinets, and eggs.'

Fay looked her astonishment. '*Eggs? Do you mean the Easter variety, or those with the little lion on the shell?*'

'Well, to be quite truthful my interest is mainly confined to pot ones.'

A dazed silence followed Bradbury's odd remark; then George cleared his throat.

'You must forgive these two, Mr. Bradbury. Their manners are inexcusable sometimes . . . I must say you interest me, though. Where do the knives and cabinets come in?'

'My husband has always taken an interest in knives — and saws too,' Vera Bradbury said evenly.

Bradbury nodded vigorously. 'Yes indeed — but mainly knives. Such interesting things! The cold steel, the light sparkling from the blade, the fine needle points. There *is* something. Sharp as a razor. All knives are not that good, I know, but those that interest me are. Wonderful things, knives! You can do so many things with them.'

Trudy swallowed hard. 'Yes — yes, I'm sure you can. What — what about hatchets, Mr. Bradbury? Have you any interest in them?'

'Hatchets?' Bradbury shrugged. 'Oh, I suppose they have their uses.'

'I assume,' George interposed, 'that cabinet making is your trade, Mr. Bradbury? You are a master-joiner, perhaps?'

Bradbury grinned broadly. 'Yes . . . ' His smile became a chuckle: 'And sometimes I'm a great *un*-joiner too, eh, Vera?'

His wife smiled enigmatically. 'Yes you are, come to think of it.'

The front door banged again. Ruth Carter came in, then paused in surprise at seeing the visitors. Quickly recovering her poise, she said: 'Good evening . . . '

'Mr. and Mrs. Bradbury, mother,' Trudy introduced. 'They want the room you've got advertised.'

Again there were handshakes. 'Delighted. Well, now . . . ' Mrs. Carter paused.

'Mr. Carter's already shown us the room,' Vera Bradbury assured her, 'and it only remains for us to come to terms. After that's done we can make all the arrangements to move in.'

'When would that be?' Ruth Carter questioned.

'Would it cause too much upset if we came tonight?' Bradbury asked.

Ruth gave Bradbury a startled look. 'Tonight . . . ' As she hesitated she noticed George nodding urgently, then: 'Well, I suppose it could be managed, though as you'll have noticed there are still one or two details to finish off.'

'Strike while the iron's hot, that's what I say,' George affirmed.

Vera Bradbury smiled. 'Naturally, we don't want to upset you, but the room will do perfectly, and we don't want to stay in an hotel. We only want bed and breakfast, otherwise we'd be out all day.'

'I see.' Ruth reflected, 'Business people?'

'In a way,' Vera Bradbury said vaguely. 'I help my husband, you see. He's — '

'A joiner and cabinet maker with an interest in knives and pot eggs,' Fay supplied.

Her mother stared. 'Pot eggs? How very odd!'

'Mr. Bradbury's a master cabinet maker on his own account,' George said quickly, 'but at present he and Mrs. Bradbury are on holiday.'

Bradbury spread his hands. 'That's it. Well, Mrs. Carter, shall we get down to business? What are your terms for bed and breakfast for both of us?'

'A pound a day.'

Bradbury nodded. 'Fair enough. Might I ask that I have nothing but water to drink? That way I keep my nerves steady. Usually, for breakfast, I like a thin slice of bacon, very fatty, and a five minute egg to go with it.'

'That can easily be arranged. Are there any other — fads that I should know about?'

Bradbury pondered, then: 'I don't think so. The fact that I drink nothing else but water doesn't apply to my wife — Oh, yes! Sometimes I get up early and meditate in the solitude of the morning.'

George wrinkled his brow, 'Are you religious, Mr. Bradbury?'

'Not particularly. Why do you ask?'

George spread his hands. 'This early morning lark. I can't think of anything else but religion being responsible.'

Ruth gave her husband a disapproving look. 'In any case, we'll fit everything in.'

'Good!' Bradbury pulled out his wallet and handed over some money. 'This is in advance. It is quite clear that we shall not be here permanently, but only for about a month?'

'I quite understand. And you are coming tonight?'

Bradbury considered. 'We're garaging the car at a place in the Uphill main street. At the moment we're parked on a side road.' He glanced at his watch. 'Time's getting on, and we've one or two odds and ends to attend to. Suppose we're back about half past eleven? Will that be convenient?'

Ruth nodded. 'Very well. Half past eleven.'

George Carter saw the couple out. He came back into the living room stroking his chin thoughtfully. 'Well, that was quick work, Ruth. You no sooner advertise than you get a result. Good! Now the never-never people will have no excuse for taking back the washer.'

Ruth frowned. 'I only wish they hadn't wanted to come in so soon. You and your strike while the iron's hot! I'm nowhere near ready for them. Between now and half past eleven we'll have to shift heaven and earth!'

'What for?' George asked, surprised. 'The room's all right.'

'It isn't all right. The floor wants a good vacuuming, and the oilcloth needs cleaning. You've made an unholy mess of it with those photographic chemicals of yours! Then there's the feather bed to be put on. It's in the kitchen at the moment — and don't mix it up with the old one. Trudy, get the vacuum and come with me.'

Trudy immediately went to the kitchen, brought out the vacuum, and went out through the hall doorway with her mother.

George glanced at Fay. 'Well, I'd better get that feather bed, I suppose. Nice job to be doing at this time of night.'

'I'll help,' Fay offered. 'Feather beds aren't easy to handle.'

'Oh, there's nothing in it,' George said blandly. 'Just a matter of knack.'

He headed for the kitchen with Fay behind him. Presently he returned, struggling with the feather bed round his shoulders, striving to keep the bed balanced and get it through the hall doorway, with Fay attempting to help. Finally they got the bed through the doorway, and tackled the stairs. Fay took the rear, with her back to the bed, but unfortunately slipped. Her rear end thumped on the stairs.

'You okay, Fay?' George enquired hoarsely.

'What do you think?' Fay said sourly.

'You go downstairs. I can manage this last bit.' George panted.

Rubbing her rear tenderly, Fay flung herself in a chair in the sitting room — only to jerk up again, gasping. Then she lowered herself — gently.

A moment later, Trudy came in, dragging the vacuum as she headed towards the kitchen. She stopped on seeing Fay.

'What's the matter with you, anyway? Lazing?'

'Lazing be blowed!' Fay replied hotly, 'I fell downstairs, if you must know! It's the last time I'll try and help with a bed!'

Trudy grinned and hurried on into kitchen. She came flying back with a bucket, heading for the hall door. But just as she reached it, bedding appeared from beyond it, hauled by a panting George.

Trudy hit it, rebounded, and dropped the bucket, before falling on top of Fay. George staggered into the room with the bed.

'Of all the damned nonsense! Why can't people say what they mean?' He reeled unsteadily with the bed towards kitchen. 'Just like a woman!'

Fay pushed angrily at her sister. 'Do

you mind? I don't want my legs amputated just yet!'

Trudy disentangled herself and struggled up. 'Sorry; I couldn't help it . . . Hey, dad, what on earth did you bring the bed back for?'

George turned towards her, swinging the bed, and nearly knocked odds and ends off the sideboard.

'It's the wrong bed!' George growled, staggering into the kitchen.

With an effort, Fay got up from her chair. 'I suppose in spite of what I said I'd better help him.'

Trudy swept up the bucket. 'Okay, get busy. I'd better get this bucket upstairs before mother goes hairless.' She exited through the hall doorway as Fay moved stiffly into the kitchen.

Ruth Carter appeared in the hall doorway. 'Where *is* the man? Doesn't take all night to bring up a bed, surely?' She headed purposefully towards kitchen, and then got out of the way quickly as the correct bed appeared, wrapped in a dust cover.

George was leading, shouldering one

end, with Fay shoving at the rear.

'Do hurry up, George! Time's getting on!'

'I'm doing my best,' George snapped. 'If you'd said which bed in the first place there'd have been no trouble.'

The bed was pushed through the hall doorway. Her lips pursed, Ruth listened to the bumps and thuds denoting their progress up the stairs. She sighed. 'I never saw such a palaver over a little thing like a bed. Hmm, I wonder if the Bradbury's will want any supper?' She began to tidy odds and ends. 'Why this place is always like a tip I shall never understand . . . '

She winced as there gave a further loud bump from upstairs. Fay's voice floated down to her. 'Hey, mum! The bed's in place. Do you want us to put on blankets and things?'

Ruth strode to the door. 'No you don't! I want the job done properly. Come down here, the rest of you . . . '

She waited until George and their two daughters all arrived, looking somewhat dishevelled. They crossed to chairs and fell into them.

'And what's the matter with you, Trudy?' Ruth demanded. 'Cleaning oilcloth worn you out?'

'Oilcloth be blowed!' Trudy said irritably. 'I've been shoving the bed!'

'Well, there's no time to laze about. Girls, tidy this room up. George, put some coal on the fire. I'll do the rest upstairs!' Ruth swept through the hall doorway.

Trudy brought in the carpet sweeper as Fay hid old newspapers under cushions. George fetched in the coal bucket, and tended to the fire.

Their tasks completed, all three slumped into chairs.

Fay frowned, 'If only I'd been able to go jiving as I'd planned!'

'Never mind,' George smiled. 'Think of the lolly!'

Trudy glanced at him. 'But it's only for a month, anyway. All this hardship for a month's lolly isn't worth the candle . . . '

Trudy was interrupted by the front door bell. She and the family got to their feet. 'That must be the Bradburys now,' she resumed. 'And earlier than they expected.'

41

3

George looked flustered. 'How do I look? I haven't even tidied myself after shifting that damned bed.'

'You'll do . . . ' Fay pronounced, after a quick appraisal.

'Everybody asleep down there?' Ruth's voice sounded down the stairs. 'Open the front door! It must be the Bradburys. I'll be down in a moment.'

Fay gave herself a quick smoothing-down, patted her hair, and then headed for the doorway.

She returned after admitting their new lodgers. 'A little earlier than we expected, I'm afraid,' Vera Bradbury apologised, noting their surprised expressions. 'We got everything arranged as we intended and we've garaged the car at the Apex Garage. I hope we haven't caused you any upset?'

'Oh, no — not at all . . . ' George lied.

Jim Bradbury appeared in the hall

doorway, carrying two big suitcases. He dumped them, beamed on the assembly, and then went out again.

'Rather a lot of luggage, and there's more spare stuff in the car to be used if needed,' his wife explained. 'There's another case to come yet.'

Jim Bradbury appeared again in the hall doorway, lugging a fairly large suitcase with a broken handle. 'Well, that's that,' he panted, putting the broken-handled suitcase on the floor in full view.

Trudy stared at it fixedly; then her eyes rolled upwards. Suddenly her knees gave way and she flattened to the floor. The others looked at her in amazement for a moment; then Ruth came in from the hall and stared blankly at the scene. 'What in the world's happened?' she demanded.

George came to life. 'Trudy just passed out. No idea why. Get the smelling salts, Fay.'

Trudy was lifted gently to the settee and given a bottle of smelling salts to hold as she slowly revived.

George shook his head. 'Queer do, that.

Never known Trudy to pass out before.'

Her mother bent over her anxiously. 'Feeling better now, love?'

Trudy propped herself, slowly, on one elbow. 'Yes, I'm feeling okay again now. I'm sorry. I don't know what came over me. I blacked out.'

George wrinkled his brow. 'Probably indigestion. It causes it sometimes.' He turned to the new lodgers. 'We hardly expected to greet you with a surprise like that.'

'I'll show you your room now,' Ruth interposed quickly. 'It's fixed up. We managed to get it done in time.' She gave a final glance at Trudy. 'Come along up . . . Oh, I suppose you'd like a bit of supper?'

Vera Bradbury nodded. 'We would rather. We've been too busy to have anything. That is, if it won't put you out too much?'

'What about Forsyth's chippy?' George suggested brightly. 'They're open till midnight. How about fish and chips?'

Bradbury beamed. 'You can't beat 'em. Very kind of you.' He followed the two women out of the room, carrying the two normal suitcases and leaving behind the one with the broken handle.

Trudy gazed at it for a moment, then got up from the settee and rubbed her arms as though she was cold.

'Get yourself warm, lass,' her father advised. He nodded towards the fire. 'You don't seem so good tonight.'

Bradbury came back, and picked up the offending suitcase. Smiling, he went back upstairs with it.

George glanced at his daughters. 'I'll go for the fish and chips,' he said flatly. 'No place for you to go at this hour of night, Fay — and I'm quite sure *you're* not going, Trudy.' Taking his hat and coat from behind the door he left on his errand.

Fay began to put out the crockery for the supper. 'Well, Trudy, what's the matter with you? You can tell *me*, can't you?'

Trudy tightened her lips. 'Even if I did you wouldn't believe me. I've said all along that Mr. Bradbury has all the characteristics of the Uphill maniac, and when I saw that suitcase with the broken

handle it just finished it. I passed out!'
She rubbed her forehead. 'Not so sure I
feel too good even now.'

Fay looked at her with incredulity. 'But
Trudy, it's absurd! I've said before: Mr.
Bradbury is a thoroughly decent chap.
Come on — forget all such nonsense and
give me a hand with the table. I'd better
lay for the lot of us, I suppose.'

'Not for me.' Trudy shook her head. 'I
couldn't eat a thing,'

Fay raised her eyebrows. 'Then you
definitely *are* bad!'

Ruth Carter led the procession, back
from the upstairs. 'Thanks for helping,
Fay. I'll put the kettle on.' She paused,
and crossed to Trudy who was moodily
seated by the fire. 'How now, love?'

'Oh, I'm all right. It wasn't anything.'

'I hate to remind you again, Mrs.
Carter,' Bradbury said. 'No tea for me.
Just cold water.'

'Yes, I'll remember.' Ruth turned to the
kitchen.

'And I wonder,' Bradbury went on, 'if
you'd mind if I had half an apple before
my supper? It helps my digestion. I see

you have some on the sideboard there.'

'By all means! Help yourself!' Ruth went back into the kitchen.

Trudy held her head in her hands as Fay busied herself arranging the table crockery, and the visitors seated themselves on the settee. Abruptly Bradbury rose, taking a big jack-knife from his pocket.

Holding it like a dagger he moved towards the sideboard. At that moment, Trudy happened to glance up, and immediately screamed.

Ruth Carter came flying back into the room. 'What on earth's the matter?'

Fay recovered her grip on the crockery she had been holding. 'You silly twerp, Trudy! What do you want to make that noise for?'

'S-sorry,' Trudy said miserably. 'Something hit me.'

Recovering from his surprise, Bradbury crossed to the sideboard, picked an apple, and began cutting it in two. He put the surplus half back on the dish and proceeded to peel the other half near the fireplace, opposite to Trudy.

47

She watched the blade, fascinated. 'Isn't that an awfully big knife for a job like that?' she gulped.

Bradbury smiled pleasantly. 'Oh, I don't know. What will do a big job will also do a little one . . . ' He tossed the cut peel into the fire.

'What do you call a *big* job?' Trudy asked, low-voiced.

Bradbury chewed his apple slowly. 'I don't know really. I find this knife useful in my work — or on a picnic. I even cut joints with it sometimes. It cuts almost anything . . . Besides, as I said earlier, knives fascinate me.' He held up the blade and eyed it critically. 'The sparkle of light from the steel, the razor thinness of the edge . . . '

Trudy stood up, holding a shaking hand to her mouth. 'Ex — excuse me. I don't . . . feel too well.' She hurried into the kitchen.

Ruth shook her head as Trudy hurried past her on her return to the sitting room. 'Wish I knew what's wrong with Trudy tonight. I'm sure the Irish stew was all right. Unless it was the onion in it

. . . Coffee or tea, Mrs. Bradbury?'

'Tea, please, thank you.'

'You having your cocoa as usual, Fay?'

'Uh-huh. Extra sweet.'

Trudy returned. 'Nothing for me, mum,' she said languidly. 'I'm not up to it.'

Ruth shrugged amiably. 'All right, love. You know your own tummy better than I do.'

Trudy returned to her seat by the fire, watching every move made by Bradbury. He put his knife away in his pocket and returned to the settee, munching his half apple.

Ruth glanced at Fay. 'I suppose dad's gone to the chippy?'

'Yes.' Fay looked up from surveying the table. 'Anything else wanted, or have I got it right, mum? This is Trudy's job as a rule.'

'You've done fine, love. And I'll bet you're getting a bit tired, too?'

Fay flopped into a chair. 'Oh, not particularly. Looks as if it's Trudy who's the sloppy one tonight.'

'Who's sloppy?' Trudy cried indignantly. 'I'm just a bit off colour, that's all!'

'I can't help thinking we've put you to an awful lot of trouble coming at this hour,' Vera Bradbury said contritely. 'Look at the time!'

Ruth smiled. 'We're often up until twelve, when we have the telly.'

'Seem to be an awful lot of murders, though,' Fay commented. 'It's always guns, poison, or a knife. Come to think of it I suppose there aren't many other ways of bumping anybody off.'

'Oh, I don't know.' Bradbury paused as he finished his apple, 'There *are* other ways, I suppose.'

'I think I'll go to bed, mum,' Trudy said, giving him an uneasy look. 'I feel a bit rocky.'

'Do just whatever you want, love . . . '

Trudy got up slowly and moved to hall doorway. She looked back at the lodgers.

'Good night. I'm sorry I disgraced myself.'

'Good night.' Bradbury and his wife spoke together.

A few moments after Trudy had left there came the sounds of the front door opening and closing as George returned, carrying a large parcel of fish and chips, wrapped in newspaper. He handed them to his wife and went to hang up his hat and coat.

Ruth quickly unwrapped the paper parcel, and threw the newspaper and grease paper onto the fire after tipping the fish and chips onto a large dish.

'Come on, everybody — draw up.' As the assembly seated themselves at the table, Ruth went into kitchen and returned with a teapot and a cup of cocoa for Fay.

'Have you any particular time you wish to be called for breakfast?' she asked her visitors.

Vera shrugged. 'Entirely up to you. We're on holiday so any time within reason suits us.'

'I should say around eight,' George suggested. 'That's our usual time. It takes me from seven to eight to get started. And that confounded fire usually chooses to be obstinate . . . By the way, where's Trudy got to?'

'Gone to bed,' his wife answered. 'If she's no better tomorrow you'll have to fetch the doctor.'

'Or somebody will.' George frowned slightly. 'Don't see why I should always be the one to be put on.'

The conversation lapsed as they all began tackling their meal, then Ruth asked: 'Regarding breakfast, Mr. Bradbury — You said very fat bacon and an egg. I don't know about the bacon. I've had no time to get any very fat stuff.'

Bradbury shrugged amiably. 'I'll settle for toast. I didn't know then that I was having fish and chips tonight.'

His wife looked up. 'Toast for me as well, Mrs. Carter.'

Fay decided to plunge. 'It's nothing to do with me, of course, but I'm curious about something.' She looked at Bradbury. 'I noticed the initials on your suitcases. One says 'A.S.' and the other 'M.K.' whilst the one with the busted handle has no initials at all. That doesn't tie up with Vera and James Bradbury, does it?'

The couple stopped eating to stare at Fay.

George sighed. 'I never knew such an

inquisitive little blighter in all my life. And Trudy's just as bad. Ignore her question. In fact, Fay, you'd no right to ask it! You see far too much, one way and another.'

'Sorry. I *did* notice it, though.'

Bradbury laughed easily. 'Well. I don't blame her for noticing. As a matter of fact they're borrowed bags. We needed them in a hurry. One of them has some special things in. The one with the broken handle. I keep forgetting to get it repaired.'

George gave his daughter a grim look. 'Satisfied, young lady?'

'Yes. Don't blame me because I'm quick on the uptake. I could ask you, why you were in such a hurry as to not be able to get bags of your own. I *could* ask, but I won't.'

'Very generous of you,' her mother said dryly. 'I never knew such inquisitiveness in all my life!'

'I've said I'm sorry,' Fay muttered sullenly.

'There are many reasons why we couldn't get bags of our own, but I've no time now to go into it,' Bradbury declared, glancing at the wall clock. 'In fact, I think it's time we packed up and went to bed.'

He and his wife got to their feet.

'Good night, then,' Ruth said, somewhat relieved. 'We'll give you a call at eight o'clock.'

'Fair enough,' Bradbury nodded. 'That is, granting I haven't decided to take one of my walks. In any case though, Vera will want waking. Good night, everybody.'

As they closed the door behind them George and his wife gave Fay grim looks.

'Any more questions like that, Fay, and you're going to kill the goose that lays the golden eggs,' George said sternly. 'Even if you are curious you've no right to ask.'

'I think I have,' Fay said spiritedly. 'I'm doing a bit of detective work.'

'You're what?' her mother frowned.

'Just looking into things . . . ' Fay said importantly. 'Why do you think Trudy passed out like a light tonight?'

'There could have been plenty of reasons.' George shrugged. 'I'll settle for indigestion upset.'

'Then you'd be wrong,' Fay said firmly.

'She passed out because of that suitcase with the busted handle, which the Bradburys have got.'

'What are you talking about?'

'She told me as much herself. Don't you remember telling me, dad, that the Uphill maniac is carrying a suitcase with a broken handle, in which are the remains of his latest victim?'

George gave a start. 'Great heavens, you're not suggesting — '

'I know it's a gory thought, but why not?' Fay was serious. 'Those two have got a broken handle on one suitcase, haven't they? Mr. Bradbury matches the description of the maniac — or so Trudy says. I think it's only coincidence, but Trudy doesn't. That's why she passed out.'

'But there must be thousands of suitcases with the handle broken at one end,' her mother protested. 'We've even got one ourselves.'

'We — we can't be giving bed and breakfast to a maniac and his wife! Or whatever she is.' George was incredulous. 'Not us! It couldn't happen!'

'It could,' Ruth admitted, 'but I hope to heaven it isn't. Oh, it's so silly! He's such a nice young man, and such a pleasant manner, too.'

'Trudy said his nice manner is also in keeping with the radio description 'deceptively charming' or something,' Fay countered. 'It makes you a bit goose-pimply when you think of it.'

George narrowed his eyes. 'I'm just trying to remember what the radio said. I seem to recall the announcer saying that a wink could start the maniac off — '

'And that the same effect would be produced by a word.' Ruth wrinkled her brow. 'But what *was* that word? I can't remember.'

'Maybe Trudy can,' Fay suggested. 'She heard the announcement, didn't she?'

George got up. 'I'll go and see — if she isn't asleep, that is.'

Fay glanced at her mother as he went out. 'What are you driving at, anyway?'

'Well, it might be a way of finding out something, and — ' Ruth broke off as the clock chimed twelve. 'Good Lord, midnight! Come and give me a hand with these pots, Fay — '

They had started to clear the table when George returned.

'Asparagus!' he said cryptically. 'That's the word we wanted. I'm afraid I upset Trudy because now she wants to know what we wanted asparagus for. If it comes to that I don't know myself. What do you think we should do, Ruth?'

'Get these pots cleared and go to bed. After all, it's all probably nonsense. Come *on*, George, lend a hand!'

Fay paused in clearing the table. 'Why didn't they put their own initials on the suitcases? And why has the one with the dud handle got something special in it?'

Ruth came back in. 'Oh, forget it. Even supposing he *is* the maniac, what should we do about it?'

'Telephone the police,' George said.

Fay shook her head. 'And we'd look a real bunch of Charlies if we were in the wrong, wouldn't we?'

At her words, everyone came to a stop, holding crockery. Then George spoke decisively.

'There's only one thing to do — take a

chance. If we're not all murdered in the night, that is.'

'Murdered!' Ruth shuddered. 'Don't be so horrible!'

George shrugged. 'If we're not all killed in the night we can try and find things out in the morning. We must be *sure* before we do anything otherwise Bradbury might sue us, and I wouldn't blame him . . . You might try winking at him, Fay.'

'Wink at him?' His daughter started. '*Me?*'

Ruth frowned. 'It's not particularly nice for a girl to wink — not the way Fay does it, anyhow. Too much mischief in her eye.'

'It's got to be done,' George said firmly. 'You wink at him, Fay, and we'll see what happens. At a convenient moment I'll try the 'Asparagus' test.'

Fay gave her father an anxious look. 'But what happens if he goes for us?'

'Don't be afraid. I'll be here.'

'Huh!'

'I'd like something more reassuring than that.' Ruth thought for a moment. '*I* know! I'll keep the pepper pot handy, within reach. That'll cool his ardour pretty quickly . . . All right, we'll try it, but I still think there's no need. Now come on — get the rest of these pots out and we'll wash up in the morning.'

The rest of the crockery was soon cleared, and the two women departed to bed. Giving a last look about him, George was about to follow them when he caught sight of the comic strip lying on the settee. He went over to it and picked it up. 'So *that's* what he did with the Empire State Building!'

He threw the paper back on the settee, gave a last look round and then departed.

4

In the dim light of the flickering fire, the sitting room clock showed 1:25. Dressed in dressing gown and pyjamas, Trudy entered from the hall doorway. She switched on the light, then yawning, she went into the kitchen, to shortly reappear chewing a bun, a second one in her other hand.

Going over to the settee she picked up the comic strip from the sofa and sat down to read it by the fire, chewing her bun meanwhile. She stiffened at a sudden sound, staring towards the hall doorway. Getting up she switched off the light, and hurried to the hall doorway, intending to get back to her room.

She gave a stifled cry as she collided with Jim Bradbury. He was dressed in trousers, shirt, and dressing gown.

'Oh!' Trudy dropped her bun to the floor, together with her half-eaten one.

'Oh, hello, Trudy.' Bradbury said

amiably. 'Did I startle you?'

Trudy backed away. 'What do you think?'

'I'm sorry. I didn't mean to disturb anybody.'

Trudy stumbled back to the light switch, and snapped it on. 'You're telling me!'

Bradbury spread his hands. 'Naturally I didn't expect to find you here.'

Trudy made her way to the armchair and stood behind it, facing Bradbury.

He looked down at the scattered crumbs made by the dropped buns. 'I'm sorry I disturbed you. You're having a snack?'

'Yes.' Trudy tightened her lips. 'I felt hungry. I didn't have any supper.'

'Then you're feeling better?'

'I was. I'm not so sure now . . . Ohh!' Trudy broke off with an exclamation as Bradbury casually brought out his jack-knife from his dressing gown pocket and snapped open the big blade. She dived blindly for the kitchen, then presently peered round the door frame.

Bradbury gave her a puzzled glance.

61

'Anything the matter?'

'That knife!' Trudy gasped. 'What — what do you intend doing with it?'

For answer he speared the remaining half of his apple, on the sideboard dish. Smiling, he held it up, then advanced to the fire. 'I intend to peel this, if you don't mind. Once I've done that I'll go.' He frowned as he saw that Trudy was passing a hand over her brow. 'Why, what did you *think* I was going to do?'

'I dunno. My nerves got the better of me . . . ' Trudy paused uncertainly, then added in a low voice: 'Why come down at this time to eat an apple?'

'For the sane reason that you came for buns. I'm still hungry, and besides apple helps me to sleep.' He commenced peeling the apple with his knife. 'This will just top things off nicely.' He looked at Trudy seriously. 'I am sorry I upset you . . . Be a bit awkward if somebody comes down, wouldn't it? We're not exactly in formal attire.'

Trudy made no answer, but emerging from behind the door frame, she slowly edged round the room, giving Bradbury a wide detour. Eventually she reached and sat on the settee.

'I often get up in the small hours for a snack,' Bradbury remarked. 'In fact I'm never in bed much before two, anyway.'

'That's a bit late, isn't it?'

'I suppose so. I make up for it in the mornings . . . '

Trudy picked up the comic strip and held it in front of her face so that she wouldn't have to talk.

Bradbury, however, seemed happy to continue the conversation. 'So you read comic strips? The one I particularly like is that one about 'Mandrake the Magician.' Who is your favourite?'

'I haven't got one.'

Bradbury finished his peeling, and shut his knife blade. Sensing Trudy's unease, he said: 'Well, I'll go. Sorry I upset you . . . Goodnight.'

'Good night.' Trudy's reply was almost a whisper.

After Bradbury had gone, Trudy put down the comic supplement and sat back in her chair. An audible sigh of relief escaped her.

Presently she got up, cleared up the buns and crumbs, then ruminated before apparently reaching a decision. She went out, only to return to the sitting room with bed sheets and a pillow.

She made herself a bed on the settee. Then, putting a chair by the bed she placed on it a carving knife she had fetched from the kitchen.

Switching off the light, she settled into her improvised bed.

★ ★ ★

The clock on the sitting room mantlepiece was striking six. The noise it made appeared to wake up Trudy. Her hand emerged from a tangle of sheets. Finally she sat up, looking about her in the dim light. Then she heard something.

Getting out of bed, she dragged the sheets and her pillow behind the settee, and ducked down herself into concealment.

Jim Bradbury, fully dressed in a light mackintosh and carrying his broken handled suitcase, came in. He switched on the light then froze, staring in surprise at the carving knife on the chair by the settee. He shrugged, then heaved his suitcase onto the table. Unlocking the catches, he snapped back the lid. He rummaged inside for a moment and there was a brief glimpse of a shapely leg wrapped tightly in adhesive tape. Nodding to himself, Bradbury shut the case lid, and went into the kitchen.

Immediately Trudy nipped from behind the settee, endeavouring to reach the suitcase. Unfortunately she became caught in a length of sheet, which tripped her up, so that she sprawled heavily onto the carpet.

The commotion brought Bradbury back in a hurry, holding a glass of water. He stared at Trudy on the floor.

Hastily she dragged the sheet up round her pyjamas and stood up.

'Hello!' Bradbury exclaimed in surprise. 'You again!'

'Hello. We seem to keep meeting, don't we?' Trudy presented a strange figure as she stood draped in the sheet, Arab-style, and appearing to peer cautiously at Bradbury from her 'burnous'.

He gave a casual nod, then drank off his glass of water at a single gulp, and returned to the kitchen.

He came back almost instantly. Trudy had not moved.

Bradbury moved to the table and clamped and locked his case. He turned to Trudy: 'I suppose I shouldn't ask you what you are doing down here at this time with a sheet wrapped round you?'

'I — I suppose I must have walked in my sleep,' Trudy improvised.

'With a carving knife?'

Trudy followed his eye to where the knife lay on the nearby chair. 'Eh? Oh, that! Must have done that in my sleep too. I remember dreaming I was about to carve a turkey.'

Bradbury gave her a critical look. 'You ought to do something about your health. It seems to be playing you tricks.' He picked up his suitcase. 'Well, I'm going for a trip. I'll be back for breakfast. 'Bye for now.'

'Goodbye.' Trudy relaxed slightly. After he had left the house, she collected the pillow and remaining bed coverings from their hiding place and dumped them on the settee. Finally she turned and picked up the carving knife. At that moment her father entered by the hall doorway, in shirt and trousers. He stopped and stared blankly at Trudy.

'What on earth are *you* doing? Playing sheiks and robbers?'

Trudy stumbled forward, still clutching the sheet. 'Listen, dad, I've seen a leg!'

'So have I, lots of times — Eh? What in the world do you mean? What are you doing here at this hour in that fantastic getup? What's the carving knife for?'

'Protection. I slept down here last night.'

'Have you gone off it, or what? Oh, wait a minute! I need to get the water for your mother's cup of tea.' George dived into the kitchen and Trudy started to fold up the bedding. After a moment her father returned. 'Now, young lady, what's all this about?'

'It started in the small hours,' Trudy explained. 'I came down to get some buns because I felt hungry. Mr. Bradbury followed me down for the other half of his apple.'

'Oh, he did, did he?' George frowned. 'It was the apple that led Adam up the garden in the first place. What do you *mean*? He came for his half apple?'

Trudy nodded, 'He had the other half before supper, didn't he?'

'Yes, but . . . ' George scratched his head. 'Oh, go on!'

Trudy shrugged. 'That's all there was, to start with, I was on the settee here, reading, and he was by the fire peeling his apple.'

'How very matey.' George's tone hardened. 'In fact too matey for my liking. Buns and apples in the small hours. I didn't think Bradbury was that sort.'

'Oh, he was quite a gentleman,' Trudy said quickly. 'Honest. He just stood there in his dressing gown and peeled his apple.'

'And how were you dressed? Like that?'

'I was in my dressing gown too.'

'You were, were you? Nice goings on!' George's tone softened. 'Good job I can trust you, even if I'm not sure of him. Well, what happened then?'

'He talked a bit about the comic strip — about 'Mandrake the Magician,' and other things, then seeing I wasn't too overawed by his company he cleared off to bed. I felt it might be safer down here, so I slept on the settee with the carving knife beside me. Then, when I woke up just after six, things began to happen.'

'Things? Such as?'

'Mr. Bradbury came down with his broken handled suitcase. He opened it, and for a moment I'm sure I saw a girl's leg wrapped up in tape or something.'

George raised his eyebrows. 'And he did all this with you watching him?'

'I was behind the settee there, peeping. He shut the case again and I decided to have a look for myself when he went into the kitchen for a glass of water. Unfortunately, I tripped over the sheet and that brought him in on the scene pronto. He seemed surprised to see me.'

'If you looked as you do now that's not to be wondered at,' George said dryly.

'I made some silly excuses which I don't think he believed. Finally he cleared out with his suitcase and said he was going for a trip and would be back after breakfast.' Trudy spread her hands. 'That's all there is.'

'And you're sure you saw a leg?'

'It looked remarkably like one. Quite a decent shape, too.'

'And how much of it did you see?'

'From the foot to just below the knee.'

George digested this information for a moment, then: 'Well, it's all a mystery to me — as much as the behaviour of Mr. Bradbury himself. Anyway, we'll try and sort it out. Now get this stuff out of here and get yourself dressed. I've got to take tea up to your mother.' He crossed into the kitchen.

Trudy collected her bedding and moved towards the hall doorway, followed by her father, holding a cup of tea. Trudy walked through the hall doorway, only to come to an abrupt halt. Her father walked into her, and dropped the tea. As they staggered about, a fully-dressed Fay came in from the hall, looking apologetic as she edged past them. Her father glared at her, then at the fallen teacup, and Trudy twisted about, trying to ascertain if any of

70

the tea had spilled onto her, whilst still clutching her bedding.

'Sorry!' Fay said contritely.

'What's going on?' George demanded. 'Do you *have* to come charging in like a blasted tornado? What are you doing down at this hour, anyway?'

'It doesn't matter now,' Fay said weakly.

'Oh, what's the use?' George stormed back into the kitchen, muttering to himself about teenage daughters.

Fay looked at her sister, relieved. 'You've taken a load off my mind, Trudy.'

'I've got a load *on* my mind, too — or perhaps you'd noticed. What are you talking about, anyhow?'

'You, of course. When I woke up and found you'd gone — and all your bedclothes too — I immediately thought of Mr. Bradbury. So I dressed at top speed and came down. I knew dad would be up and I was going to tell him something had happened to you . . . '

Trudy shrugged. 'Something did, but I'll tell you about it later. I assume I'm nor so important, really. I notice you had

71

to dress first. That doesn't suggest urgency!'

'I couldn't come down looking like something the cat had dragged in, could I?' Fay protested. 'Be reasonable! If something *had* happened, a few minutes more couldn't make much difference.'

'Oh, well! I'll get this lot upstairs — ' Trudy placed the bedding over one shoulder, but before she could leave, her father emerged from the kitchen with another cup of tea.

He handed it to her. 'Give that to your mother, and don't take too long getting dressed. We've got to lay breakfast for the Bradburys, and there are last night's supper things to wash up. Hurry!'

Trudy looked at him dazedly. 'Hurry? With *this* lot?'

Fay settled herself into an armchair. 'Wish I hadn't got up so early, only I was bothered about Trudy. I thought Mr. Bradbury had kidnapped her, or something. Then I saw the bedclothes gone, that made me think.'

'Glad something can do it,' her father said heavily. 'And there's no time to sprawl in that chair. Get some work done.'

'At this hour! But it's only seven o'clock. I don't usually turn up till half past eight.'

'I know, dressed like a queen and everything ready for you. Since you're here early for a change you can make yourself useful. Lay the table for six of us while I get the washing up done.'

Without any alacrity, Fay rose and started to set the table. She glanced towards the kitchen.

'What was Trudy doing in here, dad?'

'Staging a one-man resistance movement. She slept down here with the carving knife in case Bradbury went off the deep end.'

'Of all the idiotic ideas! She'd have been quite safe in her own bed. I was in the bed next to her if anything had happened.'

George twisted his head round the kitchen door. 'The way you sleep she probably thought a carving knife was better insurance. Frankly, I don't blame her for being a bit scared. She'd already had fun and games with Bradbury earlier in the night.' He resumed drying some plates.

'Fun and games with Bradbury?' Fay crossed to the kitchen doorway. 'Why, what happened?'

'First, she and Bradbury collided down here in the early hours. He'd come for half an apple, and she'd come for buns. They sort of kept each other at a distance — then Bradbury cleared off to bed again. Trudy slept down here after that. At six this morning, Bradbury came again, all complete with his suitcase with a broken handle, and Trudy saw a leg.'

'Whose? Bradbury's?'

'No — in the suitcase. Trudy saw it up to the knee. She bungled the job of looking in the suitcase, literally fell over herself in excitement. Out went Bradbury with his suitcase, saying he was going for a walk. And that's that.' George finished drying the plates.

Fay stepped back as he returned to the sitting room. 'It's enough too. A *leg*? How could Trudy be so sure?'

'She isn't, but it's as near as damnit.'

'Then what do we do now?'

'I think we'll have to use the wink and asparagus test.' George looked seriously at his youngest daughter. You're still game to risk it?'

'Oh, yes. Of course,' Fay answered uneasily.

George frowned. 'One thing I can't understand is that there's no smell. Remains *ought* too smell. Some kind of preservative, perhaps?'

'I know,' Fay said eagerly. 'You've got a book somewhere on the various ways of treating limbs, disposing of bodies, and so forth. I've read it, and it's a lulu. It used to be in the room the Bradburys have got. Oh, what's the name? 'Corpses Delicious'! That's it.'

'You mean *Corpus Delicti*,' George corrected.

'Do I? Well, I wonder if it could give us a hint?'

'I don't know where your mother's pitched it. Go and see her while I lay the table . . . '

Fay went out, and George went to the window and drew back the curtains. After switching off the light, he switched on the radio, then commenced to lay the table.

' . . . and over most of the country the weather will be rainy later today, with fog in parts. Outlook is for gales, snow, frost and hail.'

'Summer all over again,' George muttered. The radio announcer resumed his bulletin.

'There is still no trace of the man known as 'Moony Moses,' the maniac who is thought to have killed and dismembered Christine Ashton at Uphill recently. Reports that he has been seen in the Uphill area are being investigated. As stated last night, the police believe that the killer is carrying the head and legs of the victim around with him in a suitcase with a broken handle.'

George froze, and gulped. Been seen in Uphill?

'In Parliament yesterday — ' George snapped out of it, and turned off the radio.

Fay entered the room with a book in brown paper covers, inscribed 'Corpus Delicti by David Whitelaw'.

76

'Trudy's been telling mum what happened in the night, so I stopped to listen,' Fay said. 'I heard the radio as I came down. It doesn't sound too good about the maniac, does it?'

'We must do our best not to panic. I see you've got *Corpus Delicti* there. Where was it?'

'Mother had put it in the wardrobe next to your old Wellingtons.'

George extended a hand. 'Let's have a look at it . . . ' He put the book on the table and pored over it, Fay seated alongside him.

'Disposal by Dismemberment! That's the part we want.' He turned the pages to the appropriate section. 'Now, where are we? There's Crippen, who tied up remains in his own pyjama jackets . . . Some pyjama game that must have been!'

Fay was studying the pages alongside him. 'Look at this bit about Voirbo, the French criminal. 'He filled the head with molten lead and sank it deep in the Seine'. Ugh! 'The victim's legs were wrapped in stiff cloth and fastened with stout string . . . ' Wonder if it was cloth

Trudy saw, and not tape?'

'I only know what she said. This shows there is a precedent.'

'What's a precedent?' Fay asked airily.

'Something done or said which may serve as a sample. I *do* wish you'd paid more attention when you were at school.'

'Sorry. I couldn't do that and look after a netball team, and the boys, as well.'

'Nearly every criminal is imitative,' George mused. 'He takes the examples of some other criminal and tries to improve on it. From that we form the assumption that this maniac we're worrying over improved on stiff cloth by using tape. And I'll wager I'm right. I've studied these things, remember.'

'I see what you mean, but we still haven't got over the point of there being no smell,' Fay pointed out,

'He must be using some kind of deodorising ointment — maybe in the tape itself.'

'Beats me why he wants to carry the remains around with him,' Fay commented. 'Why not get rid of them? Be much simpler.'

George shrugged. 'Probably egomania. A maniac would have that. He likes looking at the result of his horrible deed . . . However, we're working on pure guesses, and the only thing to do is try the wink and asparagus test. He should respond to that, then we'll know what to do.'

'That reminds me! Didn't mother say something about the pepper pot?' Reaching out, Fay moved the pepper pot into an easily reachable position by her mother's chair at the table.

Her father got up, and laid the book face downwards on the sideboard. 'I think I'll get the clothesline in case he gets violent . . . ' he went out into the kitchen.

A moment later, Trudy, now fully dressed, came in by the hall entrance. 'Hmm, all set for once,' she commented, seeing the set table. 'That's usually my job, but you can have it with pleasure.' She rubbed her arms. 'It's cold in here. You wouldn't like to light a fire, would you?'

Fay shook her head. 'No, I wouldn't. In any case, I'm busy thinking.'

'About boys, I suppose?'

'No!' Fay said crossly. 'About Mr. Bradbury! Dad and I have been looking at *Corpses Delicti* and it's pretty certain that Mr. Bradbury is perhaps trying to copy another murderer — Voirbo, a French killer. Anyway, at the moment we're thinking up defensive measures for when we try the wink and asparagus campaign.'

'The *which*?'

'To draw out the killer,' Fay explained. 'Don't you see? Those two things will do it, or so the radio said last night. I didn't hear it, but you did. Remember?'

'Oh, that! Yes, I remember, but I didn't pay a great deal of attention. I'd no need to, then. I remember dad coming and asking me something about asparagus but I was half asleep . . . ' She gave a start as she realised the significance of Fay's words. 'It's a bit of a risk to take, isn't it?'

'Yes, but it's the only way to get at the truth. If he isn't the maniac, I suppose he won't respond. If he *is*, look out for fireworks.

'I don't like it,' Trudy declared. 'Simpler to tell the police and have done with it.

'And what happens if we're wrong?' Fay asked. 'We'd be the laughing stock of the neighbourhood! Bradbury would probably sue for defamation of character . . . or something.'

'Mmm, I see what you mean,' Trudy admitted. 'Anyway, what about the defensive measures? How far have you got?'

'I've put the pepper pot handy for mum, and dad's grabbing the clothesline for himself. That leaves only you and me to think of something with which to defend ourselves.'

'Right!' Trudy's eyes gleamed. 'I know what I'm having.' She got up and hurried into the kitchen, returning with the hammer with which she had earlier nailed down the mat by the door. She laid it carefully on the seat of her chair, and than dusted her hands.

'Don't know what I can use,' Fay murmured. 'I suppose I'll just have to act as the decoy.'

'Decoy?'

'The bait. I'll have enough to do just winking at Mr. Bradbury without bothering to think up a means of defence as well. In any case, with you, mum; and dad I'll be well protected.'

George came through from the kitchen, having been out in the back garden obtaining the clothesline. He put the coils on the seat of his chair and nodded to himself.

'That ought to do it. If he gets rough I'll soon have him trussed up.'

'You hope,' Trudy said doubtfully. 'If he gets as violent as most maniacs, you may go sailing through the window.'

'Have to take the risk, that's all. As far as I can see we're all ready for Moony Moses.'

Fay raised her eyebrows. 'Who?'

'That's the maniac's name — Moony Moses,' her father told her. 'I didn't know it until the radio news this morning. We'll try using his name at the right time and see if anything happens.'

Mrs. Carter entered the room from the hall. She looked the table over critically. 'There's another knife wanted, otherwise it's all right.' As Fay hurried to get the missing knife, she added: 'But what's all this stuff on the chairs? A hammer and

— My best clothes rope!'

'That's to truss up Bradbury if he gets tough,' George told her. 'Only rope I could find.'

'If it gets dirty you'll have to buy me a fresh one on Monday . . . ' she glanced at Trudy. 'What do you propose doing with this hammer?'

'Clouting Bradbary on the bonce if necessary,' Trudy said promptly.

'And you've got the pepper pot, mum, as arranged.' Fay pointed to it, as she laid the missing knife.

'I only hope we're not making fools of ourselves,' Ruth said seriously. 'If we act tough and than wc'rc proved wrong there'll be no end of a row. Bashing lodgers over the head with a hammer and then tying them up with a clothes rope just isn't done.'

'Don't worry, Ruth, everything's under control.' George assured his wife. 'He *must* react to one or other of the tests. Asparagus, winking, and Moony Moses.'

'Who's he?

'The maniac. The radio said so this morning.'

Ruth shrugged. 'Oh well I hope it works out. She gave a little shiver, 'Brr, but it's cold in here! Why doesn't one of you light a fire? I'd better go and get the breakfast ready, than we can tip off Mrs. Bradbury to get moving.' She moved off into the kitchen.

George, in his chair, was apparently meditating, whilst Fay wandered round the room tidying this and that. Trudy gave them a wry look.

'All right, I'll do it! Seems nobody else will.' In some disgust she settled on her knees before the fireplace and began preparations to light a fire. 'Get some wood, Fay, please.'

Happy to do this minor task, Fay went into the kitchen. Trudy began clearing the cinders in the grate, using the tongs. On impulse, she rescued a triangular piece of newspaper from the debris. One side of it was charred, but the other was intact. Trudy stared at it.

Fay came back carrying the firewood chips. 'There you are.' She frowned as Trudy took no notice.

Her sister was continuing to stare at the

piece of newspaper she was holding.

'Now what's the matter? Feeling funny again?'

Trudy stood up, and thrust the piece of newspaper towards Fay. 'Look — look at this!' she stuttered. '*Look* at it! This bit of newspaper — !'

5

George Carter started out of his reverie, got up from his chair and came over. 'What about it? Part of the newspaper the fish and chips were wrapped in last night, isn't it?'

Trudy nodded nervously. 'Yes. It's a corner that didn't burn . . . But look at it! You can see part of the headline . . . '

Wonderingly, Fay and her father looked over Trudy's shoulder as she held up the paper.

'See? It says . . . ' — ller still at Large!' That first word is probably 'Killer'. And here's part of Mr. Bradbury's picture directly underneath!'

'You're right,' George said, shaken. 'Dead right.'

'It *is* him!' Trudy cried frantically. 'What more evidence do we want than this? His picture — and the headlines — '

'What's that you're saying?' Mrs. Carter emerged from the kitchen, a fork in her hand.

'Corner of a newspaper, Ruth,' her husband told her. 'Killer still at large and Bradbury's picture underneath . . . Look!' He thrust the paper fragment out for his wife to see.

The fire now lit, the family began to assemble at the table. Ruth went upstairs to knock at the bedroom door of their lodgers, and call out that breakfast was ready. She returned downstairs, and stood alongside her chair, as several minutes passed.

'I do wish she'd hurry up, then we can get started.'

'I don't know that I feel like eating,' Fay said miserably. 'I've got a ton of lead inside me.'

'After *that* shock I'm none too bright myself,' Trudy admitted.

'Now listen, all of you,' George said earnestly. 'Behave normally as well as you can. At the right moment I'll confront Bradbury with this bit of newspaper and see what he has to say. We'll also try the wink and asparagus test if we have to. Otherwise, keep calm. I am complete master of the situation.'

A few moments later, Vera Bradbury, fresh and smiling, and looking anything but the wife of a maniac came in. 'Good morning, everybody. And how are we?'

Trudy gave her a weak smile. 'Oh, we're fine.'

'I'm glad to hear it,' Vera Bradbury said, sitting at the table. 'You didn't seem very well last night, Trudy. Everything okay now?'

'Yes. At least I hope so.'

'Wireless says it's going to rain,' George remarked gloomily, after a lull in the conversation.

'What a pity. And I've such a lot of things to do today.' Vera glanced at Mrs. Carter as she noticed that she was still standing by her chair. 'There's no point in waiting for Jim, Mrs. Carter. He may not be back for a while. When he goes out in the early morning he loses track of time.'

'Oh, then you know he's out?' Ruth queried.

'Of course. He told me he was going.' Vera smiled ruefully. 'Rather inconsiderably he woke me up to tell me. I'm used to that kind of thing.'

There came the sound of the front doorbell ringing.

George got up to answer it and came back ahead of Jim Bradbury. The lodger had his raincoat on as before, but there was a dark stain visible near the cuff. He was carrying his broken handled suitcase.

'Sorry I'm late,' Bradbury apologised, looking into the sitting room. 'I thought I'd be in time. Shan't be a moment.' He went out, carrying his case.

George exchanged significant looks with Ruth and Trudy, and then resumed his seat. The breakfast proceeded, and presently Bradbury returned, minus his raincoat.

'I'm glad you didn't wait for me,' he commented, seating himself alongside his wife.

'Your wife said we should begin,' Ruth said. 'She mentioned that you lose track of time when you are on one of your . . . sojourns.'

Bradbury shrugged cheerfully. 'Yes, I do. One of those things. Some people have no time-sense, as you've probably noticed.' He raised his hand as Mrs. Carter offered him the teapot. 'No tea for me, Mrs. Carter.'

'I'd forgotten. I'll get you some water.'

Bradbury stood up, smiling. 'No; you do enough running about. I'll get my own. He went into kitchen for a glass of water and resumed his seat.

There was an awkward silence, then Fay nudged her father and winked at him, at the same time giving an enquiring glance. George nodded.

'How do you like our little town of Uphill, Mr. Bradbury?' Fay asked casually.

'Oh, it's quite nice in a limited sort of way . . . '

Fay winked at him saucily.

'I find it interesting even if there is an oversupply of gasometers — '

Fay winked a second time.

' — but I suppose gasometers and industry are inseparable.'

Fay gave him a third wink.

Bradbury raised his eyebrows in astonishment, then, as Fay continued winking, he suddenly got to his feet and went across to her.

Instantly George stood up and grabbed the rope he had placed behind his back. He stood tensed, with the rope in his hands. Trudy jumped up with the hammer poised. Ruth grabbed the pepper pot and stood poised with it, ready for action.

Vera Bradbury gazed at this extraordinary tableau in blank amazement.

Bradbury, who had yet to notice these various antics, put a hand under Fay's chin and raised her face. 'Perhaps I can help you,' he said, taking out a handkerchief.

'Let her alone!' George snapped determinedly.

Bradbury released Fay and stood looking about him in astonishment. 'Why, of course . . . if you wish it.'

'What were you going to do to her?' Trudy asked sharply.

'*Do?*' Bradbury looked at her blankly. 'I was going to try and get the grit out of her eye.'

'The — the grit?' Ruth asked haltingly.

Bradbury shrugged. 'She seemed to be blinking badly with one eye, so I just thought I'd help her if I could.'

George put the rope back on his chair. 'Oh . . . I see.'

'What in the world's the matter?' Vera Bradbury demanded. 'Why are you all standing round my husband as though he's a desperate character, or something?'

'Yes.' Bradbury tightened his lips. 'I would rather like an explanation.'

'Just one of those things,' George said weakly. 'We always fly to Fay's assistance if anything goes wrong. She's easily put out.'

In the grim silence that followed Trudy put the hammer back quietly on her chair, whilst her Mother returned the pepper pot to the table.

George cleared his throat. 'Perhaps we'd better carry on with breakfast.'

'By all means,' Bradbury said in a hurt tone, resuming his seat. 'I must say that things are not quite as I'd expected to find them in a normal family, and I'm rather concerned. Not only this incident, but other things.'

'Other things?' Trudy whispered.

'Yes.' Bradbury gave her a hard look.

'You yourself, for instance. I found you eating buns in the small hours when I came down for half an apple. I found you again at six this morning looking like an Arab, with a carving knife on a nearby chair. It's all very puzzling.'

'Oh, we're an unusual family, really,' George said blandly. 'Lots of amateur dramatics rehearsals, you know. As for Trudy, she was probably rehearsing her part for the 'The Desert Song'.'

'What's she going to be?' Bradbury asked coldly. 'Red Shadow?'

'After all, everybody has queer weaknesses,' George said quickly.

'I can see that,' Bradbury said heavily.

'For instance,' George hurried on, 'take asparagus.'

'Why? It doesn't agree with me.' Bradbury resumed his breakfast.

'Then asparagus doesn't mean anything to you?' George persisted.

'Why should it?' Bradbury spoke irritably. 'I just said it doesn't agree with me. Can't we talk about something more interesting than asparagus?'

'Surely we can.' George rallied, and

produced his trump card. 'How about this?' He pulled the portion of newspaper from his pocket and held it up for Bradbury to see. 'Can you explain *that*, Mr. Bradbury? We're all rather interested. It *is* you, isn't it?'

Bradbury looked at it and then gave a visible start. So did his wife.

'Where did you get that?' Bradbury demanded sharply, looking at George and frowning.

'It's part of the paper round last night's fish and chips. It should have burned . . . but it didn't.'

Bradbury made no attempt to take the cutting. 'You're sure that's all there is?'

'Quite sure. It *is* you, isn't it?'

Bradbury shrugged. 'Oh yes, it's me, all right. Can't think how the press managed to get my photo. Oh well, can't be helped . . . What paper is it from, or don't you know?'

'We don't know,' Fay said. 'We just wanted to make sure it was you.'

Surprisingly, Bradbury relaxed and smiled. 'I suppose I ought to say 'Fame at Last'! Not that it's anything new for me to have my picture in the paper . . . ' He looked at his wife. 'Think it's a good likeness?'

Vera looked at the photograph and nodded. 'Quite good.' She glanced at her watch. 'We could make an early start for the shops and places we want, Jim.'

Bradbury nodded. 'Okay, the car's outside. Let's get ready. Excuse us, won't you?'

The Carter family looked on rather dazedly as the Bradbury's rose and went out.

George put the newspaper corner back in his pocket. 'Well, I'll be damned!'

'He couldn't have cared less, apparently,' Ruth said, perplexedly. 'We must be wrong somewhere, George. He took it all calmly and we just made idiots of ourselves.'

But George was not prepared to let the matter drop. 'What I'm going to do is find a full issue of the paper containing this photo and headline, then we'll know the truth.'

'But you don't know which paper it was,' Trudy protested.

'Yes I do. It's the *Uphill Gazette* I noticed that much when I brought home the fish and chips last night. The hard part will be tracing which issue, but they ought to have it on file at the *Gazette* offices.'

'Wonder if any of you noticed anything about Mr. Bradbury when he came in?' Trudy asked, pondering. 'There was something suspiciously like blood on his raincoat sleeve, and it wasn't there when he went out in the early hours. I remember thinking what a nice clean raincoat he was wearing.'

'Things are taking what the newspapers call an ominous turn,' George said slowly.

'And it's us that's making it so — Sssh!' Ruth broke off. 'Here they come! Look unconcerned.'

The Bradburys looked in at the doorway. Vera was dressed in outdoor clothes, with a handbag. Her husband had an overcoat on instead of his raincoat. He seemed to have recovered some of his good humour.

'We'll be back tonight, Mrs. Carter,' Vera said, 'around nine o'clock. Will that be all right?'

'Oh, certainly!'

'We shan't need any supper this time,' Vera told her. 'We'll get it outside. From now on we'll be adopting the normal bed and breakfast routine.'

Ruth looked at her contritely. 'Very well — and I'm sorry for the way we behaved at breakfast.'

'Oh, that's all right.' Bradbury smiled. 'As Mr. Carter said: 'everybody has queer weaknesses'.'

When the front door banged behind the departing Bradburys, George got up and prepared to leave the living room. 'I'm off to the *Gazette* offices and see what I can find. I'll feel more comfortable at leaving you with those two out of the way.'

Trudy spoke urgently. 'The *Gazette* can wait for a moment, can't it? The files won't alter for the sake of an hour.'

'Meaning what?'

'There's something far more urgent,' Trudy said quickly. 'Now's our chance to look inside that suitcase with the broken handle. I'll swear it was a girl's leg I saw. Let's get all the evidence and then we can tell the police.'

Her family looked at each other doubtfully.

George hesitated, then rejoined them. 'I'm not so sure that we ought to do that, Trudy. After all . . . '

'Oh, let's know where we are and have done with it,' Trudy said decisively. 'I'll get that suitcase . . . ' She hurried out.

The others began to clear the table. Presently Trudy returned with the suitcase and dumped it on the partly cleared table.

'Much of a job finding it?' Ruth asked.

Trudy shrugged. 'Not particularly. But I did notice that it was pushed well under the bed so nobody would notice it.'

The four of them gathered round the suitcase.

'Up to you, dad.' Fay looked at her father. 'You're the boss.'

'Hmm — especially when there's a sticky job to do! All right, here we go. And keep calm, all of you.' George attempted to snap back the case catches but nothing happened.

'Locked!' Trudy cried. 'We ought to

have expected it . . . ' She snapped her fingers. 'I've got a key to the office deed box upstairs, and it's just about the same size as this lock.' She studied it closely. 'Wonder if it would fit?' She hurried out in search of the key.

'I feel like a criminal doing this,' George admitted. 'We *must* be careful. If Bradbury finds the case has been tampered with there'll be a terrible row. Maybe Trudy's key won't fit.'

Fay compressed her lips. 'If it doesn't we can always prise the lock open.'

'What!' her father looked at her askance. 'And give away what we've done? Not on your life!'

Trudy returned with a key on a small circle of wire. 'Here we are! Looks as if it ought to do. These suitcase locks are never very tough, anyway.'

George took the key and began fiddling with it in one of the locks, until finally there was a decided click.

'You've opened that one, anyhow,' Fay encouraged. 'Now try the other.'

George succeeded in opening the second lock and then stood back. He regarded the case as if it was a time bomb.

'After all,' he said dubiously, 'suppose I go to the *Gazette* office first and get the paper — '

'Never mind the paper!' Trudy said excitedly. 'We've got this far, so let's finish it.'

Her father summoned up his nerve and opened the lid. After taking a quick look inside, he promptly shut the lid down again, and stood blinking.

Fay regarded him in puzzlement for a moment. 'Well?' she demanded.

As George made no answer Fay seized the lid herself, but he quickly snatched her hands away.

'No you don't! Nothing in there that you ought to see.' George paused, and moistened his lips. 'Two — two legs wrapped round and round with tape, and a brown paper parcel. A round one . . . It *could* be a head. And there's something else.'

'What?' Trudy gasped.

George gave her a grim look. 'A hatchet — bright and shining. Looks almost as though it's made of silver.'

As the implications of these statements sank in, Mrs. Carter sat down with a thud and stared at the closed case. George took the key and turned it in both locks, then he handed the key back to Trudy. Fay drifted away and stood looking at the case from a distance.

Trudy broke the ensuing silence, 'Well, we haven't finished yet. I want to know about that stain on the raincoat. I'll swear it's blood.' She looked at her father. 'You're a bit of an expert on bloodsstain chemistry, dad, so what about it?'

George made an effort and pulled himself together. 'Well, I suppose we may as well carry on. We don't want it said we called in the police without a reason.'

Trudy headed determinedly for the hall exit. 'I'll get the raincoat.'

'Take this suitcase back — ' Ruth Carter said, then shrugged as she realized Trudy had already gone. She looked at George. 'I suppose you'll want a lot of chemicals?'

'Not a lot. I only want the bendezine and hydrogen peroxide. Where have you put 'em?'

Ruth turned to Fay. 'Get them, Fay. They're on the second shelf in the wash-house.'

Fay nodded and went out through kitchen.

Ruth looked at her husband seriously. 'You're sure of what you saw in that case, George?' she asked quietly.

'Of course I'm sure! I couldn't imagine a thing like that!'

George turned as Trudy came back into the room with the raincoat. She held it forward for her parents to inspect it.

They all examined it closely.

'Certainly looks like blood,' Trudy commented, 'but it could equally be paint or chocolate. I know it's new because it wasn't there earlier.'

Her father took the raincoat from her outstretched arm and dumped the rain-coat on the table. 'Get me a piece of clean blotting paper, Trudy — the white sort.'

After Trudy had brought some for him from the sideboard drawer, George proceeded to scrape the stain with his penknife, collecting a powdery residue on the paper. 'There! That's all I want. You can take the raincoat back.'

'And that suitcase as well,' Ruth added quickly.

Trudy nodded, and took the suitcase and raincoat, heading again for the hall exit. She paused as there came a ring from the front door.

'That'll just be the grocer,' Ruth said quickly. 'I'll go . . . '

Trudy started moving again, but stopped again as she heard the voices from the hall.

'Oh, hello, Mr. Bradbury!' Ruth was saying. 'Come back for something you've forgotten?'

'No, for something I remembered.'

'Bradbury! Oh, blimey!' Trudy gasped. She scurried back to the settee with the suitcase, and just in time she managed to get it out of sight behind it. The raincoat, however, was still over her arm when her mother came in followed by Bradbury.

'We — we were just tidying things up,' Ruth stammered uneasily.

Bradbury smiled pleasantly. 'These things have to be done, haven't they?'

Trudy quickly switched the raincoat

behind her back, and began trying to edge towards the kitchen, whilst her father interested himself in the blotting paper with the powdery residue upon it.

'As a matter of fact,' Bradbury said, 'I came back for my raincoat.'

'Oh. I see!' Ruth fluttered. 'It's raining, I suppose?

'Not yet. I want to take my coat to the cleaners. I got a nasty stain on it this morning. Clean forgot it earlier.'

'Ohh!' Trudy gave a little cry as, in going backwards, she collided with the table. Inevitably the raincoat came into view.

'My raincoat!' Bradbury exclaimed in surprise.

'Why, yes — your raincoat.' Trudy stared at it blankly. 'Well I never!'

Trudy gave a wild look about her, completely at a loss as to how to explain her infraction.

At that moment Fay came in from the kitchen with two blue poison bottles. She stopped abruptly when she saw Bradbury.

Before Fay could speak, Ruth jumped in. 'Hyrdogen peroxide and — No, no, not *this* one! I can't wash your hair with *that*! Go and get the other one!'

'The other one?' Fay said blankly. 'Oh, I think I see what you mean. The *other* one . . . ' She turned and hastily exited through the kitchen.

Bradbury frowned. 'What is my raincoat — '

'Oh, yes, your raincoat,' Ruth Carter improvised. 'Well, I went to tidy up the bed and dust round and I noticed your raincoat. I decided to try and clean it for you — on the sleeve, I mean.'

'Well,' Bradbury said wonderingly, 'that was very thoughtful of you, Mrs. Carter. I wouldn't dream of putting you to so much trouble.'

'No trouble.' Ruth gave a relived smile. 'We want to be helpful if we can. Trudy had just brought it down when you came back.'

'Well, I shan't need to trouble you. I'll take it to the cleaners and let them do the dirty work.' Bradbury held out his hand for the raincoat and Trudy quickly gave it to him.

'Well, I'll be on my way.' Bradbury

looked vaguely puzzled, but by no means angry. 'See you tonight.' He gave a final smile and a nod, then went out. A moment later there came the sound of the front door closing.

'Whew!' Ruth Carter released a pent-up breath.

'That was a pretty corny excuse you made, mum,' Trudy commented. 'Wonder if he believed it?'

Ruth shrugged. 'All I could think of. He didn't seem much put out, anyhow.'

Fay's hand appeared round the kitchen doorway. 'Can I come in now?'

'Yes, come in,' George called.

Fay advanced, holding the two bottles. 'What did *he* come back for?'

'His raincoat,' her father told her. 'I'm past caring what he thought. Now we're getting at the truth it doesn't matter anymore. Right! Let's get on with the analysis.'

His family watched intently as George performed it. First the hydrogen peroxide was put drop by drop on the blotting paper; then the bendezine. The result was a dark stain.

'That's it!' George looked up excitedly. 'Blood!'

'How do you know?' Fay wrinkled her brow. 'Looks just like blue ink to me.'

'Actually it's blood. Absolute proof. The bendezine affects the haemoglobin in the blood.'

'Oh, you mean the red corporals, or whatever they call them.'

'Corpuscles!' George gave Fay an impatient look. 'Corpuscles! Anyway, here's the effect. And it's infallible. The stuff on the sleeve *was* blood.'

Trudy was struck by a thought. 'Human or animal?'

'That's the snag,' her father admitted. 'I don't know. To find out I'd have to use the rabbit test. That involves a rabbit, coagulation; and serum. It's all very complicated.'

'Sounds it,' Fay said dryly. 'Well, we've proved it's blood. Now we know Mr. Bradbury didn't get a smudge of paint from somewhere, but on the other hand he might have reached over a butcher's counter and caught his sleeve on the liver.'

107

'Butcher's shops don't open till nine, and Mr. Bradbury was in here before that,' George pointed out. 'He got the stain when he went out with his suitcase . . . Wonder if anything happened with the car?'

'I hope he hasn't . . . ' Ruth Carter's voice trailed off.

'Murdered somebody else?' Fay supplied.

'I didn't want to say that, but that's what I was thinking.' Ruth shrugged. 'You'd better get along to the *Gazette* offices, George, and see what you can find out. Once we have the final facts we'll send for the police.'

George rose decisively. 'Okay. I'll go this minute.'

After he had left, Fay collected the blotting paper and bottles from the table. 'I never thought the day would come when we'd give shelter to a murderer,' she murmured, 'Just shows you never know what's going to happen next.' She went out through the kitchen.

Ruth looked at Trudy. 'Maniac or otherwise, we'll know the facts when your father's got that paper. Now I've got to get to the shops. You know what to do when the grocer comes, Trudy?'

'Sure. I'll fix him up.'

'Not afraid to be left, are you?' her mother asked.

Trudy smiled faintly. 'I've got Fay. She's not much use, but at least I shan't be alone.'

'All right then.' Ruth Carter donned her hat and coat. 'I shan't be very long.'

6

As the front door closed behind her mother, Trudy pulled out the hidden suitcase, then settled on the settee and gazed at the case.

Fay came in and joined her. 'Where's mum gone?'

'Shopping . . . ' Trudy answered absently. 'You, know, I keep thinking about this case. We're not children any more, are we?'

'I should say not! Why?'

'Why should we be prevented from seeing what's in this case?' Trudy said deliberately. 'Dad wouldn't let us look, but I think it's time we did. We're not squeamish. We won't faint or anything.'

'Well, I won't,' Fay said. 'After last night, I'm not so sure about you.'

'I'm okay now,' Trudy assured her. 'Ready for anything.'

'All right then, you open it,' Fay invited. 'You're the oldest.'

'Yes.'

As Trudy didn't move, Fay glanced at her in surprise. 'Well, go on! Do something!'

Trudy rose slowly and reluctantly. 'All right, all right. Don't rush me.'

She picked up the case and put it on the table. Fishing out the key from her pocket, she opened the clamps.

'Ready?' Trudy looked at Fay.

'Of course I'm ready!' Fay clenched her fists.

Just as Trudy was reaching out towards the lid she and her sister jumped wildly as the front door bell rang.

'Who on earth's that?' Fay wondered. 'I nearly passed out!'

Trudy got up. 'It'll be that confounded grocer. I'll go . . . '

Fay stood looking dumbly at the case, then turned at the sound of voices from the hall, followed by heavy feet pounding upstairs. Trudy came flying back into the room, manifestly worried.

'It's Bradbury again!' she exclaimed.

'What! What does he want, this time?'

'This case!' Trudy fumbled with her

key. 'He — he said something about wanting his case with the broken handle. Then he dashed upstairs to get it.' Lacking time to lock the suitcase, Trudy decided to simply clamp it. 'Quick!'

She whirled the case under the settee and Fay quickly sat on settee, arranging her full skirt so that it hid everything under settee.

Bradbury came into the room. 'Sorry to butt in, girls, but have either of you seen my suitcase? The one with the broken handle?'

'You — you mean the one you had last night?' Fay stammered. 'The — the one — one you came back with at breakfast?'

'That's it. Do you know where it is?'

Fay shrugged. 'Why, no. How should I?' She picked up the comic strip from the settee and began reading it, casually — but her hands were shaking.

Bradbury looked at Trudy. 'And you've no idea?'

'Don't you know yourself where you put it?'

As Bradbury took a step forward, Trudy backed warily round the table.

'Yes, I know perfectly well where I put it,' Bradbury stated deliberately. 'Under the bed behind the other suitcases. But it isn't there now! I want it in a hurry. I've got the car waiting at the end of the street.'

'It's strange.' Trudy spread her hands. 'Very strange.'

'It's more than strange.' Bradbury frowned. 'I wonder, since your mother decided to clean my raincoat if she also — '

Fay put down the comic strips and sprang up from the settee. 'Don't you start hinting things about mum, Mr. Bradbury!'

In jumping up Fay had overlooked that her skirt no longer hid the suitcase.

Bradbury strode towards her, pushed her to one side, and proceeded to drag the suitcase into view. He looked at it, then at the two girls.

Trudy had positioned herself so that the table was between her and Bradbury. 'Now I wonder how that got there?'

Fay hurried across to her sister's side.

Bradbury flung the case on settee, then

turned to the girls, his lips compressed. 'Don't pretend ignorance, either of you! You know perfectly well how it got there. It was *brought*, and you — ' he broke off as he discovered that the catches were unlocked. 'Good Lord, this is a bit much! Who's been unlocking this case?'

The sisters hung onto each other and didn't answer.

Bradbury became annoyed. 'I asked a question, and I expect an answer. *Who's* been tampering?'

Trudy found her courage. 'The game's up, Mr. Moony Moses, if you only knew it! And don't try anything, either.'

Bradbury stared at her. 'Try anything?' he repeated. 'Why should I? And what's the idea of the 'Moony Moses' monicker?'

Trudy looked about her uneasily, and her gaze moved to the seat of the chair she had used at breakfast. On it there was still the hammer. Next to it was the clothes rope on the chair her father had used. She smiled grimly to herself, then cried out:

'Action, Fay! Grab that rope!'

Before the astonished Bradbury could

help himself, the girls sprang on him. Trudy hit him over the head with the hammer and he collapsed, half dazed, in a chair by the table. Fay got busy with the clothesline and secured him to the chair.

Bradbury slowly recovered, and looked blurrily at Trudy as she stood over him, dusting her hands.

'Well, that's that! Who said girls were the weaker sex?' Trudy glanced at her sister. 'Nothing else for it with our lives at stake, but I wish mum or dad would hurry back — '

She broke off as the doorbell rang. 'Oh! That confounded grocer!' She went through the hall doorway.

Fay listened to a mumble of voices and then gave a start.

'Mrs. Bradbury!' she gasped, and skipped to the hall doorway, whirling up the hammer as she went. She waited by the door, then as Mrs. Bradbury entered, she hit her across the back of the head.

Vera reeled in anguish, clutching her head.

'Quick! Haul her to the sofa before she falls down!' Trudy directed.

Between them, the sisters steered Vera Bradbury over to the settee, where she sank down, slowly recovering herself, whilst Fay stood at the ready clutching the hammer.

At length, Vera Bradbury had recovered somewhat. 'What *is* this?' she demanded. 'A home for delinquents? I came to find out what's keeping Jim and you hit us over the head! Ouch, but it hurts!' Wincing, she gently rubbed the back of her head. 'What do you mean by tying my husband up like that? What *are* you? A couple of maniacs?'

'Reverse the charges, and you'll be about right,' Fay snapped.

'Reverse the — What are you talking about?' Vera glared. 'Are you daring to suggest my husband and I are maniacs?'

'We're not so sure about you,' Trudy admitted, 'but we are about him. Moony Moses himself!'

'But this is crazy!' Vera protested. 'I never heard such rot! I thought you were both too old to start playing cowboys and Indians. There'll be plenty of trouble about this, believe me. We'll have the police on you!'

'That's a good one,' Fay said sourly. '*You'll* have the police on *us*!'

Bradbury slowly opened his eyes. 'Oh! Ow, hell! What hit me?'

Trudy smiled grimly. 'I did, Mr. Moony Moses.'

Bradbury stirred, then realized he was bound. 'Mr. Moony — ? What are you talking about?' He gave a start as he saw his wife slumped on the settee. 'Vera! They didn't attack you too?'

'What do you think?' Vera winced again as she felt gingerly at her head. 'I've got a lump the size of a potato on the back of my head.'

Bradbury glared angrily at the two girls. 'You confounded young lunatics! What's the idea?'

'You know as well as we do,' Trudy told him.

'But we don't!' Bradbury yelled. 'Get these infernal ropes away from me!'

Fay shook her head vigorously. 'Not likely!'

Bradbury relaxed helplessly. 'What's all

this about? I simply ask who has been tampering with my suitcase, and then you attack me. You're a mighty queer family! I haven't got over that rope and hammer business at breakfast yet!'

'You're staying bound up until my father returns,' Trudy said implacably. 'Then he can get the police, Mr. Moony Moses!'

'Will you stop calling me by that idiotic name?' Bradbury panted furiously.

'You shouldn't object to it,' Fay told him. 'After all, it's your own name.'

'My own name?' Bradbury spoke dazedly. 'But — but — I give up!'

Vera was staring at the suitcase beside her on the settee. 'Jim, did you say they'd been tampering with this? I thought *you'd* put it here.'

'I did, but it was under the settee to start with, and the locks were undone. Somebody had taken it from the bedroom. I was asking how it happened when these two set about me.'

Vera glared angrily at the two girls. 'How *dare* you open this suitcase?'

'We haven't done yet, but dad has' Fay

was unrepentant. 'He's seen inside it, but it was something so horrible he wouldn't let Trudy or me have a look. Or mother either. We were going to look on our own account when you interrupted us, Mr. Bradbury.'

Bradbury's manner changed. 'Wait a minute! Let me get something straight. Did you say there is something horrible in that case?'

Trudy nodded vigorously, 'Definitely. The only mystery is: how did you kill the smell?'

'Eh?' Bradbury looked blank. 'Smell? What smell?'

'Dead bodies, or parts thereof, usually pong.' Trudy frowned. 'Only you seem to have stopped it somehow.'

'Look, girls, there's something awfully haywire somewhere,' Bradbury said anxiously. 'Else you're crazy. Satisfy yourselves. Open the suitcase.'

The sisters hesitated, looking at each other.

'Go on,' Bradbury urged. 'Open it!'

'Do you think they should?' Vera looked anxiously at her husband. 'Wouldn't that give too much away?'

'I don't think so — and anyway we can't have this nonsense about dead bodies and things.' Bradbury looked imploringly at the Trudy and Fay. 'Go on, girls — open up.'

'On second thoughts,' Trudy said doubtfully, 'it had better wait 'til dad gets back.'

'Untie me, and let *me* show you!' Bradbury implored.

Fay was suspicious. 'So that's the idea, is it?'

Bradbury was becoming exasperated. 'Vera, open it for them.'

His wife looked doubtfully at Fay who remained standing with the hammer poised.

'Let her do it, Fay,' Bradbury said. 'Promise you won't hit her.'

'All right . . . ' Fay was still doubtful. She backed away slightly from Vera.

Vera opened the case as the girls watched nervously. From it she extracted two model legs, and placed them on the table. The legs were the type used to display stockings, and wrapped in white tape for protection.

The legs were followed by a brightly shining hatchet. Last of all Vera unwrapped the brown paper circular parcel and extracted an ordinary play ball.

Fay and Trudy crept forward to look at the table.

'There!' Vera unwrapped the tape from one of the legs. 'Satisfied? Was it worth assaulting my husband and me for *this*?'

'You two must have had a very real reason for the way you behaved,' Bradbury said thoughtfully, noting the sisters' contrite expressions. 'I'll swear you're not vicious really.'

'Of course we're not,' Trudy said quietly. 'We were just trying to protect ourselves from a maniac.'

'What do you mean — maniac?' Bradbury was still puzzled. 'You don't think *I'm* one, surely?'

'I'm blowed if I know what to think,' Fay admitted frankly. 'But, what *is* all this stuff, anyway? The ball, the legs, the hatchet?'

Bradbury considered, then he gave a shrug. 'I suppose I'll have to tell you if there's ever to be any peace, but you must promise to treat it in confidence. First of all, untie me.'

'Well,' Trudy said doubtfully, 'that takes a bit of — '

She broke off as the front door suddenly banged. Seconds later her father came into the room and gave a violent start as he took in the scene. 'What's been going on?' he demanded.

'Mr. Carter,' Bradbury said patiently, 'will you please try and talk sense into these two daughters of yours? I'm half dead with cramp and I've been attacked with a hammer. So has my wife.'

'You've *what*?' George Carter's jaw dropped. 'But I never heard of such a thing!'

'It was very necessary — or seemed so at the time,' Trudy said defensively.

'Get that rope from Mr. Bradbury at once!' George commanded.

'But, dad — ' Fay began.

'Do as you're told!' her father snapped. 'Hurry up!'

The front door banged again as Mrs. Carter returned. On entering the room she looked round amazedly.

'What in the world — ?' She put down her carrier full of parcels.

'Mr. Bradbury came close to attacking us because his suitcase had been unlocked,' Trudy said defensively, 'so to save ourselves we attacked him first.'

'Attacked him?' Ruth raised her eyebrows. 'That was a bit extreme, wasn't it?' She moved to the table and looked at it. 'What's all this stuff?'

Fay began untying Bradbury. 'That lot's out of the suitcase.' Her voice rose in annoyance as she turned and looked at her father. 'I blame you for most of it, dad. Not allowing us to see inside or anything. Just a couple of dummy legs and a rubber ball. What's so horrifying about that?'

'I didn't look long enough to make sure,' George shrugged. 'The rubber ball could have been a head.' He glanced at Bradbury as he struggled to his feet. 'You're feeling all right, Mr. Bradbury?'

'I'm okay, but I think these two ought to be put under lock and key!'

'I've thought that many a time,' George

said heavily. 'However, I think you'll forgive them and my wife and I when you know the facts.'

He pulled a newspaper from his inside pocket and held it out. It could now be seen that the 'Killer' headline and the photo of Jim had no connection. The name of Arthur Smart was under the photo of Jim Bradbury and the 'Killer' information was all in the column at the *side* of the photo.

'I think Mr. Bradbury, it would be easier if I used your real name,' George said. 'It's Arthur Smart, according to this paper.'

'Well, yes. It is,' he admitted.

'And your wife's maiden name?'

'Margaret Kirby.'

Fay snapped her fingers. 'The 'A.S.' and 'M.K.' initials on the suitcases! They fit!'

'Exactly!' George nodded. 'The name 'Bradbury' and 'Vera' are assumed, but I'd like to know why, Mr. Smart.'

Ruth was having difficulty understanding the revelations. 'But who *is* Mr. Bradbury? What's all this about?'

124

'Mr. Bradbury, otherwise Arthur Smart, is a well-known stage illusionist, who recently performed a special trick,' George explained. 'He performed it as a try-out before the Magic Circle, and then mysteriously disappeared. 'Arthur Smart' is the caption under this newspaper photograph. It refers to him as being missing.'

'Arthur Smart? Arthur Smart?' Trudy repeated. 'I seem to have heard that name quite recently somewhere — *I* know. On the radio last night. It was an item that you switched off, dad.'

'A radio announcement about *me*?' Arthur Smart looked at Trudy in surprise.

'Yes, it said something about there still being no news of Arthur Smart, the young man who recently astonished theatrical circles with — Blah — blah. It switched off there.'

'Suppose,' Smart suggested, 'before I explain myself, you tell me why you all behaved so queerly?'

'Simple enough,' Fay said. 'We mistook you for Moony Moses, the Uphill maniac.'

'Well, thanks very much.' Smart frowned.

'Why should you? Do I look like a maniac?'

'Anything but,' Trudy admitted. 'That's what had us bothered. But the radio said a man about five foot ten, with black hair, blue eyes, and carrying a suitcase with a broken handle, in which were the remains of his victim. What would *you* think? We'd already got the breeze up — *I* had anyway — and a glimpse of what looked like a woman's leg finished it.'

Smart was grinning broadly. 'So that was it! As your father has said, I'm an illusionist, in the midst of perfecting one of the neatest tricks for some time. I found at the Magic Circle that I needed modifications to the trick, and needed a quiet spot. An hotel wouldn't do — I'd be too well known, and reporters are the bane of my life. So I chose a quiet spot far from home — Uphill, to be exact. I disappeared from London, taking my wife with me. We've only been married a month, which is why the suitcase initials haven't been altered yet. Neither of us have any parents living, so in that direction we knew there'd be no enquiry. But evidently some of our friends have

126

become concerned over us, hence the newspaper photo and radio report. I can assure you I'm no maniac. I just want quiet in which to experiment.'

'We ought to have guessed,' said Fay ruefully. 'You said you were interested in cabinets, pot eggs, knives, and all the things magicians specialize in.'

'And have you found quiet?' George asked.

Arthur Smart nodded. 'An hour ago my wife and I found a small ground floor warehouse, which will do for a secret rehearsal room. That's why I came back for the old suitcase containing my props.'

Trudy was still curious. 'Where did you go with that case in the early hours of this morning?'

Smart shrugged. 'It was a nice morning, so I went to practice in a quiet field before anybody was around. I was prepared to do that as long the weather held good, but now we have a sizeable warehouse room it won't be necessary. It's essential nobody should see this trick of mine in rehearsal. It would ruin everything.'

'His act is called 'Woman in Quarters','

Margaret Smart put in. 'It's the most brilliant trick ever. I ought to know. *I'm* the woman.'

George raised his eyebrows. ''Woman in Quarters'?'

'The effect is that a woman is covered with a sheet. Then with four blows of a hatchet she is apparently reduced to quarters — each quarter being distinct and separate. It's a vast improvement on the 'sawing a woman in half' gag. These props are all I need when I rehearse. The ball, as you suggested, takes the place of the head. More than that I can't tell you without giving things away.'

'Then that's a stage hatchet you've got there!' Trudy said wonderingly. 'That's why it's so bright and shining!'

'That's right,' Arthur Smart confirmed. 'A lot of the secret is in the hatchet. However, please don't say anything to anybody, despite inquiries about me.'

'You can rely on it,' George assured him, 'and we for our part seem to have made complete asses of ourselves. It wasn't entirely without reason, though. The Uphill maniac is still on the loose somewhere.'

Fay had been listening attentively, but still wasn't entirely satisfied. 'There's one other small item, Mr. Brad — Mr. Smart. Trudy says that when you went out in the early hours you had a clean raincoat on, but when you came back there was blood on your sleeve, and we know it was blood because dad made a test. How did it happen?'

'Quite simple. I went in the car this morning, as you know. When I got out into the country I ran over a rabbit. It went at such a rate I didn't stand a chance. I got out to investigate and found there was nothing I could do. In picking it up I must have got some of the blood on my sleeve.'

'So much for the bendezine test!' George sighed, 'I must improve it to include animals in future — '

He paused as the front door bell rang.

'That must be that confounded grocer that you've been expecting all day,' Trudy said, glancing at her mother. 'I'll go, mum.'

As Trudy went out to answer the front door. Mrs. Carter looked contritely at her lodgers. 'Well, both of you, I hope you won't hold it against us for coming to the wrong conclusion.'

Arthur Smart smiled. 'Of course not. In fact we'll . . . bury the hatchet. There's been deception on both sides if it comes to that. When we return to London, our disappearance can be used to make good publicity — '

He was interrupted by a wild scream from the hall. All eyes looked towards doorway as Trudy came flying back.

She was plainly terror-stricken.

'There's a man on the doorstep!' she gasped. 'I thought he was a hawker! His suitcase led me to think so . . . It's got the handle broken and — '

She broke off as through the hall doorway there lurched a dishevelled-looking man, holding in his hand a massive hatchet.

He grinned ferociously as the Carter family and their lodgers all dived for safety.

Slowly, the maniac came forward . . .

Chamber of Centuries

We came over the brow of the hill at twilight. Back of us was the last dying flush of the summer sunset, ahead of us the sprawling, ill-organized little township of Calford. Somehow, the sight of the place came as a shock to me.

After the happy days of marriage and honeymoon, the whirlwind travel in and between cities, it was exceedingly depressing to find the journey's end a shambles of makeshift shops and houses, dominated on the eastern side by a solitary residence in its own grounds.

'That the place?' I asked Jane, as our car coasted down the long slope.

She gave a quiet nod but did not speak. I had noticed that expression of gloom on her usually bright young face for some time now. Her dark eyes stared sombrely through the windscreen,

'Well, anyway, you sure didn't exaggerate when you said the place was gloomy,'

I murmured presently. 'But I still think it's a lot of bunk — about the phantom, I mean. There aren't any such things — '

She turned on me suddenly, just as she always did when I derided her notions on spooks.

'It's true enough, Dick! Oh, why did you have to insist we come back to make sure? We could have made our home in New York as you suggested, and I could have sold this old place. We — '

'Now wait a minute, Jane! I'm not having my wife going all through the rest of her life haunted by a crazy memory. I'm going to prove to you that it's simply your own imagination that has conjured up the ghost theory. We're going to stay in this old place of yours for the rest of the vacation, and before it's over I'll prove how wrong you are.'

She gave a rather bitter smile. 'All right. But you'll see . . . '

I sped up through the town and in five minutes was driving up the elm-lined entrance to the residence. The trees were in full foliage, wet and sticky with summer evening dew. Jane rang the doorbell while I unloaded our bags from the rumble seat.

A thin, dark-eyed woman with skin too tight for her bones opened the door and gave a little exclamation.

'Well, Miss Jane! Glad to see you back . . . Good evening, sir,' she added, as I came up the steps.

We spent a few moments in introductions. The woman was the housekeeper, Mrs. Baxter. With her husband, who was odd-job man and general factotum, she kept the place in general order. My inner thought was that it must be a pretty lonely job. Old Baxter himself, who took the car into the garage, was strong for his age, grey-haired, and with a certain hard fixity of expression, which I could not like.

When we sat down to dinner in the immense and rather chilly dining hall Jane asked Mrs. Baxter a question.

'Has anything happened? Has — has *he* appeared yet?'

The woman shook her head. 'Not yet, Miss Jane. It's only the twenty-first of June yet, you know; *he* only appears on the longest day — tomorrow.'

Jane nodded moodily. I saw Mrs. Baxter hesitate for a moment, then she went on earnestly:

'Why don't you leave, Miss Jane? Why don't you get out of this place? Take that offer from Chicago and sell the place. Don't worry about Tom and me. We'll get fresh places. You're married now, and a young wife like you oughtn't to be in a gloomy old place like this.'

'Good advice, and she'd probably take it except for me,' I put in calmly. 'It was my idea to come back here, and I'm stopping here until I lay the family ghost. Once that's done, we're leaving anyway. I believe you folks have lived here so long the place had gotten into you — but not so me. I've led a city life and no ghost in existence can give me the jitters.'

Mrs. Baxter eyed me steadily for a moment, a queer look on her face. Then she shrugged her shoulders and went out without a word.

'Listen, Jane,' I went on quietly, 'I want the whole truth on this. So far, you have only given me snatches. What is the real dope on this family phantom?'

'It dates back to Eighteen Hundred,' Jane said, pondering. My great-great-great grandfather was Sir Jonathan Melrose, an English lord. He was a great traveler, journeyed to various lands, made plenty of friends and also plenty of enemies. The enemies he made mainly by practical jokes, which were not infrequently pretty alarming, even dangerous. Anyway, he made Hampshire, the English county where he resided, too hot for him by one of his stunts. He had to quit England — but rather than do just that, he decided to take his residence, the Elms, with him. So he had it transported to America here, stone by stone, and rebuilt. In those days there was no village in Calford, of course.'

'So I imagine. What happened then?'

'His enemies followed him to America, so the record reads, and killed him in his bedroom upstairs. In a letter he wrote just before his death — which he seemed to realise was imminent — he said that his presence would forever haunt the room and that he would return in person on the night of June 22nd at seven in the evening, in every year thereafter until the house should be demolished. Certainly his presence is always noticeable in the room. There is an atmosphere of the grave in that locked chamber in the east wing.'

'And he had appeared at the times predicted?'

'All save three occasions. He has become a legend. Successive generations have seen him, successive generations have been appalled by the mystic forces in the room. My father and mother knew of them. I have known them just once. I have grown up with the legend, and the truth was passed on to me two years ago when my father died. My mother died when I was born, as you know. It was after father's death that the Baxters came in to look after things. I went away for a while. I rambled round to different places, met you, and — Well, you know the rest.'

'This bedroom you speak of has always been locked up?'

Jane nodded. 'Except for investigations by professional followers of psychic phenomenon. They've said there *is* psychic power in that room. No person can stay in it above three minutes without collapsing.'

'Charming place,' I murmured, and Jane looked at me seriously.

'Now you know why I want to get away, why I was so against us coming back here.'

I patted her hand gently. 'I'm only doing it to eradicate the fear of the unknown which has been with you ever since you were a child,' I told her slowly, 'I don't believe for a moment that Sir Jonathan actually returns. Anyway, he's an original ghost,' I added, grinning. 'Most of them come about Christmas time; he chooses midsummer! Nice going!'

'Honestly, Dick, it isn't a joking matter,' Jane said going on with her dinner rather huffily. 'You'll find that out tomorrow, when he appears.'

'How long does he stop as a rule?'

'About three minutes, then he fades as mysteriously as he appears.'

I went on eating, thinking hard. So Sir

Jonathan had been a practical joker, had he? Maybe this was a posthumous trick beating anything he had done during his life. I started putting odds and ends together. Jane, mesmerized by the constant superstition of the place, could not see things as detachedly as I could. It struck me as queer for a ghost to turn up at midsummer, and even queerer for his presence to turn any body crazy at any time of the year. I did not credit the psychic implications. No ghost, surely, would fix the date and time of his coming so accurately?

'Well?' Jane asked quietly, and I started from my preoccupation.

'I'm going to have a look at that room tonight before the old boy shows up.' I stated quietly.

She gave a sigh. 'All right — but I'm warning you it's dangerous. I'd much rather you didn't,' she added earnestly, getting up and coming round to me.

'There's no other way to start an investigation.' I pulled my fountain pen flashlight from my pocket and tested it. 'Come — let's be looking.'

She hesitated for a moment, then seeing I was determined, she led the way from the room and up the broad, ancient stone staircase to the upper floor. We passed down a long and exceedingly drafty corridor to the east wing.

Immediately we got to it, I felt my spirits start to sink. There was something peculiar about this section of the old residence. It was more than gloomy, it was positively sepulchral.

'That's the door, third along,' Jane said, straining to keep her voice steady. 'The key is in the lock, as it has always been. Please be careful Dick — *please*!'

She clung to my arm tightly as I moved along. I wished my resolution had not so depleted itself in the journey from downstairs. The corridor we were in had a broken window at one end. Beyond it, the elm trees were motionless in the summer evening gloom. Outside, crickets and night life were making the devil of a row. Under our feet lay a thick carpet of dust — the dust of centuries since this wing of the house had been completely abandoned with the beginning of the appearances of Sir Jonathan.

At last we stopped outside the third door. The key was coated in rust and left red streaks on my fingers as I turned it. It made a noise like a corncrake. The squeak of the old-fashioned but still useable lock, and the further scrape of hinges as the door swung inward, sounded like thunder in our tense, expectant ears.

I heard Jane breathing hard, I felt her try ineffectually to pull me back. The pair of us stood motionless on the threshold of the room, my small light flashing an investigatory beam in all directions. The beam was not steady, for I was trembling. It was not so much because I was frightened but because my nerves were all shot to pieces. Jane too, was dithering like a jelly.

The beam revealed a floor thick with dust, stirred into a fine haze in the air. Place was stuffy too, long sealed. There were three windows of heavy stained glass, thickly dirty. Outside it seemed that rain had washed them into smeary streaks.

The rest of the room contained exceptionally old-fashioned furniture thick with dirt. There was a four-poster bed, a wardrobe, chairs, several other oddments. I began to move into the centre of the room, leaving Jane in the doorway.

The moment I got into the middle of the room something happened! It was just as though all the demons of hell suddenly leaped out at me and seized my vitals. A wave of intense dizziness made my head spin like a top. I dropped my torch and cried out at the same time. Unnameable horrors lurked in the gloom. I felt bestial emotions surge through me. In two seconds of time I was changed into something hunted and demoralized. My sanity was being whipped away from me by unknown forces. Hammering, beating horror flooded my brain . . .

Wheeling round, I saw the oblong that was the doorway and blundered toward it. I literally fell through it with Jane clawing at my arms. She slammed the door of the room and turned the key . . .

Slowly, very slowly, the horrible thoughts

receded from my mind — but I felt like a wet sack as I got to my feet, knees trembling, perspiration streaming down my face. Covered as it was in dirt and cobwebs, I must have made a sorry picture.

Jane turned a sheet-white face to me.

'Now you see?' she whispered.

'I see — but I don't understand,' I replied unsteadily. 'There is *something* in that room, sure — but it's got to have a logical explanation.'

She stamped her foot hysterically. 'Oh, Dick, why don't you realiase that the room is genuinely haunted? There are no explanations for such things! One — one just accepts them.'

'Yeah? Well, I'm not going to!' I was feeling confident again now. I took her arm and we went downstairs together. As we went, I did some more thinking.

'Considering everything,' I said slowly, when we were back in the sitting room, 'I'd say we both suffered from some sort of nervous depression — intense depression, conviction of horror such as assails a chronic neurotic or a potential suicide. In the centre of that room, reason was nearly blasted out of me.'

She looked at me gravely. 'It's not for us to dabble, Dick. It's some sort of evil presence. I'm sure of it!'

'Old wives' bunk,' I grunted. 'Just the same, I admit it wants thinking over. Nothing more we can do about it at the moment so let's get to bed and reason it out in the daylight. Come on.'

We passed Mrs. Baxter on the stairs and she eyed us steadily.

'Everything is prepared,' she announced. 'Will there be anything more?'

'Nothing,' Jane said. 'Nothing at all, thanks. Goodnight.'

I watched the old girl go down the staircase and was pretty sure that she kept her eye on both of us all the time we went along the upper landing. I glanced toward that deserted, windy east wing and shuddered. The memory of that awful room died hard . . .

★ ★ ★

It was close on one in the morning when a slight creaking sound in the corridor outside awoke me. I sat up, listened. Though I could not be dead sure it had sounded like softly treading feet.

'Jane! Jane, wake up,' I shook her gently.

'I heard it,' she responded, rising up beside me. 'I haven't been asleep . . . Somebody creeping about. But why?'

'Soon find out,' I retorted. 'Grab some clothes.'

As we dressed hastily, I searched round for some kind of weapon. The heavy fireplace poker was all I could discover — and there was my heavy flashlight if need be. Thus armed, I stepped out into the silent corridor with Jane beside me. Like wraiths we crept down the cavern of stairs. In the hall there did not appear to be anything unusual. The old grandfather clock was ticking solemnly.

'I suppose it must have been the Baxters?' Jane whispered.

'Guess so. Couldn't have been anything else, could it? But where are they?'

She thought for a moment. 'Perhaps in the cellars,' she said quickly.

'There are dozens of them sprawled

round under this place.'

'Lead on,' I said, holding her arms.

We went across the hall to a door under the staircase. It was swinging open.

'They're down here, right enough,' Jane muttered. 'Be careful. Mask your light.'

The spotlight revealed a flight of stone steps. When we had reached their bottom, Jane led the way with some nervousness through caverns of stone, some of them still stacked with cobwebby bottles of wine, others filled with all manner of junk, until we came to one in which reposed a locked door, on the further wall. But there was a light under that door!

I doused my torch immediately and Jane clutched my arm.

'Must be the Baxters — but what on earth can they want down here?'

We moved to the door together and pushed it gently. It was solid teak and firmly locked. For a moment we stood puzzling, listening to strange metallic clanks and thuds from within the cellar. So thick was the door, no sound of voices penetrated.

'A mirror,' I said softly. 'That's what we want! Can you grab one?'

'This do?' She took a tiny minimizing mirror from the compact fitted to her dress belt. I lowered it to the crack at the door base and stared into it. But I did not see much to help me.

I got a narrow focus vision of what was beyond. I could see two pairs of feet, a man and a woman's, together with a collection of metal rods on the floor, and an oil lamp. That was all, except that one of the rods was stained with curious, darkly glistening substance.

Jane looked after me, then shook her head. 'Got me licked,' she sighed.

'We'll look at the place when they're out of the way,' I said finally. 'For the time being, let's move. They won't know we've been down here after them, I don't suppose. Come on.'

Back in the safety of our room, we looked at each other grimly.

'Can't make it out,' Jane said, frowning.

'I'd give plenty to find out if they're connected with that chamber of horrors on the east wing,' I muttered.

148

'Can't be — in the cellar. No connection. No, they're up to something quite apart from the horror room. This whole place crawls with mystery. I begin to think it would be a good idea to sell it and be done with it.'

'Was that what Mrs. Baxter meant at dinner time when she referred to that offer from Chicago?'

Jane nodded. 'There's a man willing to buy this place for a building scheme. Says pulling the place down will kill all ghosts anyway. Not that that worries him. He wants to put up a block of flats here.'

'Here?' I echoed. 'Out in the wilds? And he's in Chicago?'

'He buys up lots of places all over the country. He offered two thousand dollars for this.'

'What!' I yelped, aghast.

'With ghost,' Jane added seriously. 'Maybe the mechanics of business are too deep for me, but it seemed a good price — '

'Gypping, with murder thrown in,' I retorted. 'No, we'll do a bit of ghost-laying ourselves without the help of

Chicago, thanks. The ghost should turn up tomorrow anyway. So, until tomorrow night we'll lie quiet and give the Baxters no reason to suspect anything. Right?'

She nodded slowly. 'All right. But I still think it would be better to sell . . . '

* * *

Jane and I spent the next day idling about, doing nothing to attract attention, though I did feel pretty sure the Baxters had some notions up their sleeve. I even had my suspicions that they knew we had followed them the previous night. Maybe we'd left footprints in the cellar dust. Anyway, though quite respectful in their behaviour, they were rather chilly. Mrs. Baxter in particular had difficulty in keeping herself amiable as she served first lunch and then dinner.

There had unfortunately been no opportunity of getting down secretly to that cellar, and to have sent the Baxters away from the house on some pretext would only have served to arouse their suspicions and perhaps precipitate something.

150

Altogether, it was a pretty melancholy, depressing day.

But at last it drew to a close. At a quarter to seven I said briefly to Jane: 'We'd better be getting upstairs.'

The long beams of the sinking sun were cast in bars across the east wing corridor when we reached it, revealing it in all its grime and dilapidation. We hesitated outside the door of the horror room, then I turned the key and flung the door wide, backing away immediately.

A faint sensation of horror began to grip me. My knees started to tremble. Jane actually cried out and clutched my arm.

'Steel yourself!' I panted. 'We've got to see this thing through this time. Hold on!'

She nodded rather desperately and stared with me into the chamber. It looked rather different, with the sunlight glancing into it. The stained and blotched walls, for instance, were covered in many parts with fleshy-looking nodules, something I had not observed last time by flashlight. Nothing else was changed. My small light still lay where I had dropped it.

The conviction of horror seemed to come in waves as we stood there, but its force was nowhere near that existing inside the room itself. We both stood trembling helplessly, watching as the sun moved from the third window to the second, then to the first and last, illuminating half its dirty length. Down in the hall, the grandfather clock chimed seven strokes with disagreeable solemnity.

Suddenly Jane gripped my arm — but I knew already what she meant. Something was forming in the middle of the room — the vague, misty outline of a man's figure. The spectacle was decidedly uncanny in the half-light, especially with the wafting waves of horror beating round.

'Dick, I can't stand this,' Jane panted, white to the lips. 'It's too awful!'

Just the same she did not go away. She was too fascinated for that.

The figure increased in density with the moments and finally took on the quite discernible impression of a man of middle age, attired in old-fashioned clothes, one hand dramatically out-thrust.

I stared at it blankly, hypnotized — then, at a sudden unexpected sound, we both whirled round. Baxter was right beside us, a gun in his hand.

'Jane!' I yelled, whirling her to me, but I had no time for more. Baxter jumped forward, seized the pair of us and bundled us into the room, slammed and locked the door on us.

Wild terror roared into our brains immediately. Jane screamed with sheer bodily anguish and I felt my head spinning. Obscene thoughts, vile urges, clattered through my mind, and that damned ghost stood staring at me, pointing. Jane dropped to the floor, unconscious.

Chattering and muttering to myself, laughing insanely for no reason, I charged at the ghost. I went right through it and collided violently with the wall. My hands slapped into those rotten fungoid growths and snapped them off. An overpowering stench, and with it increased madness, surged to my brain.

Instinctively I pinched my nostrils to shut out the smell — and became aware of something clse at the same time. The

153

horror abated a little. Weakly I staggered to the window, slammed my fist right through it. The stained glass smashed — and with it the ghost vanished! I stared stupidly, comprehending vague notions. The cool evening wind blew gloriously in my face.

I caught Jane up, hauled her inert form to the window and smashed out the remaining glass. She lay in my arm, gulping, slowly recovering. With the fresh air, the horror slowly receded, left us weak and trembling.

'The ghost.' Jane whispered. 'It's gone!'

'Yeah — and I think I know why,' I retorted. 'In fact, I think I've tumbled to the whole rotten set-up in this room. Come on — outside. I've things to ask that swine, Baxter.'

We got through the window onto the low-built road running beneath it. It was not particularly difficult to reach our own bedroom. Once more I picked up my handy poker and crept to the door.

I opened it just as footsteps came hurrying along the landing. It was Baxter, obviously racing back from the east wing after being sure we had got the full benefit of the room's horrors. When he saw me, he slid to a stop, hesitated momentarily in amazement, then fired.

His aim went wide because I hurled the poker at the same moment. It struck him right across the hand and brought a yelp of anguish from him. In one leap, I'd snatched his weapon from the floor.

'Not so smart, eh, Baxter?' I snapped. 'Jane, phone for the police from the bedroom.'

She turned back to comply, and while she was at the instrument Mrs. Baxter appeared on the top landing, started violently. But I'd seen her.

'Come here, you!' I shouted. 'Beside this precious husband of yours!'

They backed to the wall and stood waiting, grim-faced.

'They're coming,' Jane said, behind me.

'Good.' I looked at the Baxters steadily. 'You can save yourself a lot more trouble by spilling everything. What's in that cellar?'

Baxter smiled bitterly. He knew the game was up. 'So it was you two that followed last night. I figured as much.' He shrugged. 'Oil,' he said briefly.

I whistled. 'Now I begin to figure things out! You mean the rods were for a test bore?'

'Yeah. Worked properly, there'd be a gusher. We figured to drive the girl out, have the property bought cheap, and go to town. We knew from charts of the district, there was oil somewhere around here — that's why we came as servants. We knew about the ghost legend too, and decided to play it up for all it was worth to drive Miss Jane out — '

'You deliberately arranged all that?' Jane shouted hotly.

'Not all of it,' I said grimly. 'The ghost was actually caused by a tiny figure in the stained glass, wasn't it? Just as stained windows embody little cherubs, angels, so forth.'

Baxter nodded sourly.

'Guessed as much when I put my fist through it,' I breathed. 'I know now why Sir Jonathan stipulated the 22nd of June. It is the longest day, and the only day likely for the sun to reach that particular window. The climate is fairly reliable so the effect would not often miss. You see, Jane, it was a little image in the glass, obviously put there by Sir Jonathan as one of his jokes or whims. The sun acted like a carbon arc and projected a photo-like picture on the dust always floating in the room. Sir Jonathan may have intended to frighten his enemies, but instead he succeeded in scaring his descendants.'

Jane shook her head. 'But the windows were dirty,' she cried. 'How could — '

'Possibly you saw to it that that image was kept clean, eh Baxter?' I demanded.

'Yes, damn you. All we wanted to do was frighten Miss Jane out — but tonight I was desperate and — '

'But the horror of that room?' Jane whispered.

'Fungoid growth,' I said. 'They give off some sort of gas which, when inhaled, is a tremendous depressant to the nerves. Queer sort of fungoid. It's name, I believe, is *barinuth* — sometimes called the Climbing Toadstool. It's a South American plant and grows in shady places in damp. It gives off an odour, which affects the nerves and brain. Sir Jonathan, a world traveller, probably picked it up in his travels and added it to his ghost idea. Its roots are in the cellar and it grows up between the walls. Damned ingenious — '

I broke off and glanced up sharply. The sound of an approaching police siren came clearly on the night air.

The authorities gave the Baxters five years apiece for their crimes. I kept my word to them and soft-pedalled their attempted murder. They were, I felt sure, more fools than rogues, and I did not want to have too much on my conscience.

We had the oil checked by experts. That was a year ago.

Anytime you wish, you will be welcome at the Melrose Oil Concession, and if you ask for Jane or me you can have the verification of the story I've told. We live in New York now, however. The old house with its jinx was destroyed to make room for the gushers, and with it went the mystical chamber of centuries, which had nearly bereft the girl I love of her reason.

Ice Maiden

'Now, sweetheart, you stay here and play with your toys. It won't be long before I'm back . . . '

Vera Morton's nurse took a last, fond look at the merry-eyed child in the nursery, and then she went out and locked the door. Possibly Ella would have been more loyal to her charge had not spring been in the air as it was, the only thing which mattered to her was a date in town with a certain dashing young Lothario.

Vera Morton was just six years old, plump and black-haired. Also in town, her mother and father were attending an important social event . . . And below the Morton flat, directly under the nursery in fact, David Gregory toiled steadily with complicated apparatus. He surveyed the accumulation of equipment with satisfaction — the coils, condensors, insulator-banks, and loops of flex socketed to power points.

The click of the door latch made him glance up, and his young son William came strolling in, hands in pockets, interest written all over his youthful face.

'How's it coming on, dad?'

'Oh, not so bad . . . ' David Gregory gave a smile and ruffled the boy's shock of hair. 'Will, you're eight years old now, and unless I miss my guess you'll be the son of a millionaire before you're another eight years older . . . '

'Better be before that, Dave . . . ' Gregory's wife came in and closed the door. 'This luxury apartment which you've transformed into something resembling a garage needs paying for, remember. Either that invention of yours works, or we go on the rocks . . . Landlords are funny that way.'

'It'll work, dear,' Dave Gregory assured her earnestly. 'In fact, I don't think there could be a more perfect system for military defence. All a matter of getting the War Office to see eye to eye with me. Close the switch, and out goes a field of energy, which stops any invader getting within miles of us. That means directed missiles, too. Nothing whatever can get through a field like this: even A- and H-bombs would be dissipated.'

'Yes, Dave,' his wife said patiently, quite at sea.

'I'll show you what I mean,' he volunteered. 'Watch!'

He made a final check-over and then threw the master-switch. Instantly a tremendous pressure-wave surged through the room. It was followed by a terrific explosion that hurled David Gregory, already dead, clean through the window. His wife collapsed, blood streaming from her battered head. Young Will was swept off his feet and slammed senseless against the wall —

The entire building rocked.

But this was not all that happened. When young William, still living, had been rushed to hospital and the building was searched, the nursery of Vera Morton overhead was found to be intact. Door locked, windows shut — but of Vera herself there was no sign. The child had utterly vanished, nor did she return despite the frantic efforts of her parents to trace her. There just did not seem to be the vaguest clue as to how she had disappeared, or of her present where-abouts.

Gradually, the mystery of Vera Morton found its way into the files of unsolved problems, and the years passed by . . .

★   ★   ★

Will Gregory grew up with the remembrance of that sinister explosion rooted in his brain, and the death of his father and mother sharpened the remembrance. Once he left the care of the State to make his own way in the world his one aim was to find out exactly what his ambitious father had been driving at.

Will was now twenty-one, and even more scientific than his father had been. He was the owner of a small television, radio and electronic gadgets shop. In the back region of the shop, at night, he endeavoured to reconstruct the apparatus his father had made, piecing things together from the faded plans which had been left to him from the flat's few salvaged possessions.

'Some kind of energy screen,' Will muttered, brooding over the plans and partially reconstructed apparatus. 'It looks from this as though his basic idea was to shift the molecular foundation of matter and thereby cause a warp, or change, in — '

He looked up sharply, frowning. It seemed as though somebody had come into the shop for there was a distinct draught blowing. With a grunt of impatience Will turned towards the shop inter-doorway and then checked himself.

'You crazy?' he asked himself. 'You locked the shop up half an hour ago!'

As he stood pondering his momentary lapse he heard a sound exactly like a window closing. Puzzled, he rubbed his head and waited for he did not know what. Then he turned back to his pile of electronic components — But damnit, there *was* a draught, and a cold one too for a very mild night in the early autumn

'You're getting soft, m'lad,' he murmured, throwing himself in the chair to study things out . . .

After a while he had decided upon a definite course of action. He got up, picked up the screwdriver, and then started to work. He hesitated in wonder as he felt the hairs on the backs of his hands tingling oddly. His knuckles, too, felt stiff and cramped and the draught from nowhere had swiftly and mysteriously increased. Giving a little shiver he pulled his coat from the back of the nearby chair and got into it quickly. As he did so he glanced casually at the thermometer and nearly dropped the screwdriver in his amazement. The thermometer's mercury had nose-dived to below freezing point!

Of course, the thing was impossible. Temperature just couldn't drop that quickly. He went across to the electric heater and switched it on; then turned to look through the slowly glazing window. Through the clear patches — for he had not drawn the curtains — he could see people walking about casually enough, and there was certainly no sign of frost.

Slow wonder settled on Will. It changed to alarm as he felt an unearthly aura growing round him — a tightening, biting cold that gripped every nerve.

The machine on which he was working? Perhaps it — No; that had nothing to do with it. The machine was not even switched on.

'Yet if it isn't the machine,' he said out loud, 'what the hell is it?'

'*I* am responsible, Mr. Gregory, if it's the cold you're talking about.'

'Huh?' Will swung round and stared blankly at the radio, thinking that for a moment some queer coincidence had supplied the answer to his musing. Then he realised the radio, like the machine upon which he was working, was not switched on. Yet he could have sworn somebody had spoken —

'You can't see me, Mr. Gregory, but I can see you quite clearly. Maybe you can feel my presence, though?' And as Will stood goggling at the emptiness cold such as he had never known bit into him like a buzz-saw. He gasped with the stinging pain of it and then relaxed helplessly against the window frame.

'I gather you do feel it,' the calm voice commented.

With difficulty Will found speech.

'What — what is this? Some damned silly game? Some trick because I'm alone here experimenting? I heard you come through the window a little while ago, and if it's you, Molly, with one of your practical jokes — '

'My name isn't Molly: it's Vera Morton. Does that name mean anything to you?'

'Vera . . . Morton?' There was a long silence as Will wrestled with the incredible. 'But — But Vera Morton was the kid who vanished from the flat above ours years ago!'

'I was the kid!' came the retort: 'I've grown up since then. I'm nineteen years of age.'

'For the love of heaven what is going on?' Will demanded in bewilderment. 'If this is some psychic manifestation I'll get the proper authorities to deal with it . . . But frankly, I don't think it is,' he continued, his tone changing. 'We'd get on a lot better if you'd bring out the concealed transmitter and refrigerator and called it a day. I've work to do!'

'You'll listen to me, Mr. Gregory! If you have doubts about my really being present take a look at this!'

Will turned slightly and then stood watching in amazement as inside the adjoining shop he saw small boxes and empty crates suddenly flake with frost, then rise into the air and hurl themselves several feet. Other objects rapidly iced over and capered about like the creations of a séance.

Something was there, then — invisible, diabolically cold, hurling things around by some kind of physical volition.

'Now do you believe it?' the feminine voice demanded. 'I tell you I am Vera Morton, and I am the same girl who was blown into another plane by some infernal invention just over thirteen years ago — No, stand where you are! If you come too near me I might kill you with the cold. I may even do that anyway in the finish, but first I want to give you a chance to speak . . . Sit down!'

'But — I — ' Will gazed blindly into space.

'Stop bleating, can't you, and sit down!'

Will obeyed, and waited. The voice

seemed to be speaking from the store, about five yards distant. Frost had gathered round the spot where the girl now presumably stood.

'Now listen,' she continued deliberately. 'I know exactly who you are because I have spent a long time looking for a relative of that crazy inventor, David Gregory. From information from various sources — and no place is barred to me, remember — I have been able to discover all about the explosion, all about the death of my parents, and their frantic and useless searching for me. Now I have found you. I have studied you, and I want justice. As the son of the man who got me into this mess, you have got to get me out! I hope you realise what has happened to me?" The girl's voice rose in anger.

Will shrugged. His first alarm had gone now.

'You seem to forget that you're invisible to me,' he said. 'How can I realise what's happened to you when I can't even see you?'

'That's just it! The fact that you can't see me! I'm shut out from my own world because of what your father did to me with his insane meddling!'

Will sighed. 'Seems to me you're jumping to conclusions. I don't see what my father did to get you into this condition. As a matter of fact I am trying to reconstruct his apparatus in an endeavour to find out what he intended. As far as I've got up to now it looks as though the experiment had something to do with a plane of force — '

'Plane of force!' The girl's voice was derisive. 'I'll tell you what he did!' Will shivered with cold as the girl came closer her voice quivering with emotion. 'The radiations from his machine must have travelled upwards in a straight line. You, your mother, and your father simply got the explosive effect — but in the room above I got the full radiation onslaught. All I remember was being absorbed into a grey fog whilst my body was racked and twisted as though it were being torn to bits. Then the fog cleared and — Well, I'll never forget it! I was in a strange land, a child in an unknown plane.'

'Then?' Will ventured, as there was

171

silence for a moment

'I was taken care of by the people in this plane, but kind though they have been to me they still are not human beings. In fact, judged from human standards, they look pretty repulsive. All I can do is look out onto a world they can never see and consider myself labelled as a freak. I'm shut out, consumed by an overpowering longing to mingle with my own kind! And why? All because of your father!'

'My father didn't know what he did,' Will answered quietly. 'Please believe that. Incidentally. There's another side to the picture. Don't you realise how unique you are? Speaking from the scientific angle you are a masterpiece of — '

'Never mind the scientific angle! As far as I am concerned, I am simply a human being locked in an alien plane of existence. Because of my normal birth I retain enough of my natural physique to enable me to see into this plane — your plane, that is — which is something the beings of this other world can never do, any more than you can see the place where they dwell. I can also hear what is going on in this world of humans, and that is how I learned to talk and read above the mere vaporings of a child of six. There are other things too. I can see heat waves, radio waves, cosmic waves . . . '

'It's incredible!' Will whispered.

'Not to me. As a matter of fact, it seems pretty clear that your father — unwittingly maybe — proved Heinsenberg's Principle of Indeterminacy. This, stated briefly, means that the electrons of matter do not so much exist as concrete things but as probabilities, as liable to be shifted out of their positions as a mist is dispersed by a breeze. Nothing is, Mr. Gregory: all that exists is the probability that it is. Well, then, the vibration from your father's machine changed the entire probability make-up of my body. Understand?'

'Vaguely. Keep on talking.'

'The probability that I existed as Vera Morton in a world of humans yielded abruptly to the probability that I existed as Vera Morton in a plane of matter contiguous to this one. Molecules vibrate at a given speed, but your father's machine's radiation changed all that and transplanted me from one plane to the other. Not by actual physical transportation, but by altering my molecular vibration to the extent that I lost 'sympathy' with my normal plane and instead vibrated in 'sympathy' with this other one.'

Will did not say anything. By this time he was lost in thought, grappling with the theory the girl was postulating. It hung together too, especially so when based on the Principle of Indeterminacy.

'You can never contact this plane,' the girl resumed, 'because you pass through the people and substances in it. Likewise they in regard to you. It is a simple matter of differing vibrations, which actually is all there is to any material structure. For years I have been lost in this other plane. It was only as I became older that it dawned on me where I really belonged and I set out to find the reason for my plight. I have, with the scientific resources my friends possess, made my body a little more normal — but I could only get so far. I have become solid enough to walk and see, and hear and talk, in this human plane, or I can see into my own plane as well by a slight optical effort. But I am not visible in this human plane! My molecular rate is so slowed down that I don't radiate light waves back to you, and also because of that slowness I am surrounded by an aura of intense cold. Everything I touch here turns to ice! Somehow I've got to get back!'

'Just why did you come to me?' Will asked. 'You could not possibly have known that I had any plans left of my father's machine.'

'No, I didn't know.' The unseen girl was quiet for a moment, then: 'As a matter of fact I came to exact reprisal.'

'Quite candidly, I don't blame you — but it's a bit unfair to blame me for something my father did. I was only a child too, then, remember.'

'Much of what you have said, Mr. Gregory, makes me believe that the whole thing was an accident in the first place, but as your father's son it's still your job to try and get me back to normal. Find out precisely what your father did and then reverse the process. And don't try anything likely to hurt me or those who've befriended me or I'll hit back hard!'

'I don't see any reason for that tone!' Will objected, getting to his feet. 'I'm all for you, not against you. How could my father have known, anyway? Why on earth should he want to blow a six-year-old child into another plane? Be reasonable! As to your other-world friends, what reason would I have for wanting to hurt them?'

'Silly of me,' Vera Morton confessed, sighing. 'But from what I have seen of men they're a greedy, destructive lot when they have science in their grip. I've become so that I trust nobody after the raw deal I got early in life . . . Anyhow, carry on with your work and I'll visit you again soon.'

And suddenly there was an icy breeze and Will watched stupidly as frost crept up the panes of his shop's door glass. The bolts shot back apparently of their own accord, then the door opened and presently slammed shut. A warmer air began to settle.

'I'll get you back,' he breathed. 'Yes, I'll get you back, if only to find out what you look like!'

He reflected for a moment on the odd fact that he did not know a single detail about her — except her voice, and he was willing to admit that he had liked this immensely.

He looked down at the pools of water where the frost was thawing; then he turned back to his job with new resolve.

* * *

Vera Morton's icy presence did not make itself felt for some days afterwards, but Will pressed on just the same in the reconstruction of his father's machine. A week later he felt he was far enough advanced to make a test. Giving the apparatus a final look-over he switched on the juice and waited uncertainly.

'According to this setup, the energy-field should pass through the transformers and be released in an ever-widening area — But that isn't right! Damnit, it's simply radio transmission in a novel form. It's no more a field of energy to deter an invader than my foot!'

He frowned, realising he had got things completely wrong somewhere. His instruments revealed clearly that he was generating radio short waves — but nothing more. Unusual radio waves, certainly, and with a microphone he could have had a passable 'ham' station.

Switching off again he fiddled around, examining the details and getting more puzzled — then he looked up sharply as a familiar icy draught blew about him.

'Oh, it's you again!' He looked into space, still unable to absorb the fantastic wonder of the situation.

'Yes, it's I.' For some reason Vera Morton's voice was bitter with fury. 'I should have known I couldn't trust you! Like father, like son, eh? You try and kill my friends in this other plane — in fact you have killed some of them — just to show how smart you are! Why do you have to do it? What have they done to you?'

'Done to me? Why — nothing!' Will was trying hard to grasp what she meant; then he jumped back with a gasp as a searing cold flame seemed to come near him. In amazement he watched the humming apparatus become dead as a frost-glazed switch moved of its own accord and broke contact. Then the girl's voice came again.

'I warned you, Mr. Gregory, that if you tried to harm me or those who have aided me, I would take reprisal. I'm going to do just that! I don't know your reason for attack — maybe fear of invasion from this other plane, which is quite impossible if you'd only take the trouble to think it out. But in any case I'm going to make you smart! I'll make this whole city smart, in fact — '

'Hey, wait a minute!' Will cried. 'I just don't get what you mean! I *am* trying to help you — honest! I want to meet you, see you as you are, find out all about you — '

'You'll find that out very soon.'

'Hear me out, can't you? I haven't managed to get this apparatus right yet, but I will do. I'll bring you back to normal, I promise, but you've got to give me time in which to do it. As for trying to kill anybody in your plane, it's just frankly ridiculous.'

'Ridiculous, is it? You stand there and tell me that when you've generated a wave that means death to them? I don't believe you! All radio waves are visible to me, and to my friends here, but they don't do us any harm. Now you have invented a new type of short wave which is death to my friends and near-death to me because I am partly back to normal human form . . . You've murdered several of my friends, and that demands reprisal.'

'But how was I to know? Radio waves don't affect human beings: you must realize that. I never suspected — '

'You're telling lies! You must know that radio waves can hurt under certain conditions, else you wouldn't do it . . . But you won't get away with it!'

The cold suddenly ebbed from Will. He turned, rather stupefied, and watched the familiar frosty journey through the shop. The door opened and shut.

'Of all the damned, crazy . . . '

Furiously he swung back to the apparatus, and then he paused, his eyes narrowed in thought.

'I must keep reminding myself that I'm dealing with a girl who has no idea of the extent of the gulf between us. She has been brought up to see the very things which we only know of by instruments.'

He shrugged and tried to thrust the remembrance of her threatened reprisal out of his mind. He worked on steadily — one hour, two hours. Then he came to a halt, the whole thing crystal-clear in his mind.

'Got it! The output load is altered by the fifth cadence, which shuts out the upper field . . . Great heavens, that *would* be a field of shattering power, with a vengeance! Matter itself would buckle up or else change its makeup. That must have been what happened to dad. He only half did the job, blew up the works, and shifted Vera Morton's molecular makeup into another plane. Just the way it happened, and it could have been any scientist. That it happened to be dad was just too bad.'

He considered for a moment or two, then continued with the job, taking the entire formula to pieces bit by bit, reversing its whole action. And by degrees fatigue began to get the better of him and he started to doze —

* * *

He awoke shivering in every limb to find a grey daylight struggling through the frosty window. Blowing on his cramped blue hands, stamping his feet, he twisted his head to look at the thermometer.

Overnight it had dropped below the zero mark! It came as a shock to him when he realised that but for the heater, which was still operating, he might have frozen to death whilst he slept. The change in the weather was far beyond the normal for the autumn.

Reprisal? The thought began to creep unbidden around his mind as he recollected Vera Morton. Was it possible that she was in some way responsible for this, or was it just a local condition confined to this workshop?

Will got up and hurried through the shop. Opening the door he looked outside. A wind like the edge of a razor blew into his face. He saw a sheet of glassy ice where road and pavement had been. Overnight, the normal dew must have condensed into ice as fast as it had settled. What few people there were about were moving slowly, clinging to railings and shop fronts to save themselves from falling.

Puzzled, Will turned back into the shop and dragged on his overcoat. He turned on all the available heat and then set about gathering together some breakfast from the tinned rations he always had on hand. No sense in going to his rooms: he would have to open the shop soon, anyway. To shave, wash, and brew tea was impossible with every tap jammed with ice. In the end he had to gather broken ice from the cold water cistern and melt it in the kettle.

At noon he switched on the radio news

bulletin and for the first time gained some idea as to what had happened.

' . . . and this morning finds the whole of southern England in the grip of a severe cold spell,' said the announcer. 'It is considered curious in official circles that these arctic conditions are limited to southern England, the remainder of the country enjoying comparatively mild weather. The main weather bureaus are at a loss to understand the development since their charts do not reveal the presence of any cold front, or an anti-cyclonic system, which could bring in cold waves from the north or the Continent. Around two o'clock this morning the temperature dropped to thirty-four below zero. Rivers are now frozen, harbours ice-locked, reservoirs sealed; and hundreds of people have died from exposure and the sudden change. It is possible that it may be a climatic freak, confined to one area, and scientific experts are studying this factor. It is known that arctic conditions can be produced over a large area by artificial means if necessary. Some criminal blundering upon this scientific possibility might make use of it for his

184

own ends — to paralyse the life of a community, for instance . . . '

The announcer paused and then went on to a different topic. Will switched off, blew on his hands, then returned to his apparatus. But he just could not get Vera Morton out of his mind. She was back of all this somewhere. If only she would return and give him a chance to explain . . . That was not very likely, he realised. Possibly the only way to recall her was to get the apparatus so perfected that she could be restored to normal.

So throughout the day Will went on working steadily, only twice disturbed by customers since few people were venturing outside. By evening he had got the reversal process pretty well worked out in theory — Then he looked up in surprise as there came a sudden imperious hammering on the locked door of the shop. Puzzled, he went to open it and found himself gazing at two men who had the air of police officers about them. Such a possibility was substantiated to Will when, glancing beyond the two men, he saw a patrol car parked further down the ice-glazed street.

'I'm a police officer, sir,' the taller one announced, displaying his warrant card. 'I have here a warrant to search your premises.'

'What the blazes for?' Will demanded blankly. 'What do you suppose I'm doing? Counterfeiting money, or something?'

'Take a look around,' the taller one said, with a nod to his companion.

'Hey, wait a minute — ' Will hurried after both men as they marched through the shop into the rear regions. 'What's the idea of busting in on me like this?'

Neither man answered. He followed them into his workshop and waited in silent wonderment whilst they surveyed his apparatus. Then the taller one switched it off and turned a grim face.

'You own this apparatus?' he asked briefly.

'Certainly I do! But — '

'What's your name, sir?'

'William Gregory. And I may as well tell you — '

'You can save all that until later. You're under arrest, Mr. Gregory. We got this wavelength at headquarters on the detectors just before the freeze up began, and

186

we've been watching for it coming again. We got it again tonight from the same place — here! You've some explaining to do. Get your things on.'

'But, officer, this is absurd — '

'Move! Bring that stuff with you, sergeant.'

Will looked around him helplessly; then he donned his coat and afterwards sat in silence as he was driven over the glassy roads to the nearest police headquarters. Finally he found himself in the dreary office of the Superintendent.

'Look here, Superintendent, I've got rights in this matter!' Will snapped, thumping the desk. 'You have no right to hold me on any charge, or search my place as you did — '

'We had every right to search your place, Mr. Gregory, otherwise the warrant to do so would never have been issued. As for the charge against you, it follows automatically. We could have charged you last night only we wanted to be sure before picking you up — '

'But what is the charge?' Will nearly yelled.

'Causing general public alarm. It's the freeze-up.'

Will stared. 'The — the freeze-up?'

'We all know this freeze-up isn't natural,' the Superintendent explained. 'We know that somebody is causing it deliberately through scientific means. The presence of a new type of radio wave, two nights on the run — which type of wave could produce atmospheric changes — is quite enough for us. Do you deny, after what was found on your premises, that you have a new design of radio apparatus?'

'Of course I don't deny it. But I do deny causing the freeze-up. Why on earth should I want to do that?'

'That's for you to say, isn't it? If your apparatus is perfectly harmless, why not tell us what it does? It'll make things easier for you at the trial.'

'Trial?' Will gave a start.

'That's what I said. It is an offence to use radio apparatus of new design without a Government test first, especially one liable to upset the public. Get it through your head, Mr. Gregory, that over two hundred people have died from this cold wave, and the cost in money and hold-ups presents a tidy item, too. If you've got an explanation to help prove your innocence then let's hear it. Our scientists will go to work on it for you quickly enough.'

Will remained silent and shook his head slowly. It was just commencing to dawn upon him that he had no alibi at all. The story of an invisible woman, or that of a radio apparatus designed exclusively for the destruction of matter, would never be credited by the matter-of-fact police.

'So you're not going to say anything?' the Superintendent asked bitterly.

'No.'

'It'd be best for you to think it over, Mr. Gregory, because you're in an exceedingly tough spot. All right, boys, take him away.'

Still dazed, Will found himself escorted from the office and before long he had been bundled into a cell, upon which a barred door was noisily clanged . . .

★   ★   ★

189

For a reason which Will was at a complete loss to understand, he found next morning that the ice had thawed considerably and there was a warm wind blowing through the ventilator of his cell. The ice hold-up was over.

On the face of it, it looked as though Vera Morton had called off her reprisal — unless the freeze-up had been the overture to something far worse. In any case, Will was under no delusion now as to how things looked for him. The scientists would be taking full note of this thaw, were perhaps even now taking his machinery to bits and finding explanations, which, damnably enough, were there plainly enough! The machine could be proven to emit radio waves capable of producing cold: that was the devilish part of the whole business.

By and large, Will spent a restless day. It was around midnight again when he became aware of a chilliness coming into his cell. He jerked upright on his bunk, his heart pounding. Quickly he moved to the barred window, and then he fell back as the glass suddenly cracked. Immediately afterwards there followed a series of taps by something unseen and the broken pieces of glass were quickly removed.

Biting cold surged in upon Will. He shivered, but continued to watch the performance with fascinated interest, the details only dimly revealed by the solitary lamp glowing in the ceiling of the cell. He saw the strong bars of the frame coat with hoarfrost; then they began to glisten with ice. Colder and colder still the air became. Then gradually the window bars began to change their nature and powdered away into grey ash.

'Mr. Gregory! Will Gregory!' The familiar voice of Vera Morton was calling urgently, but how different it sounded! It was no longer harsh and impersonal; instead it was almost apologetic. And it was the first time the girl had used Will's Christian name, too.

'I'm here,' he answered. Then he added: 'Take it easy! Don't come into this narrow cell or I'll freeze to death!'

'I know that. You noticed what happened to these bars when I held onto

191

them? It shows very clearly the gulf there is between us, doesn't it? Anyway, listen carefully, because I haven't got very long. I'm perched on the stone ledge outside here and I don't know how long it will hold me because of the cold I'm radiating. It's quiet enough out here so when I've gone drop down into this alleyway and I'll join you.'

'Wait!' Will moved as close to the invisible girl as he dared. 'I'm wondering what made you come after me and give me the chance to escape. How did you know I was — '

'Tell you later. Follow me the moment the frost has thawed from the window sill.'

Will fancied he heard the sound of her body dropping to the narrow little street back of the prison headquarters. He waited, thanking his lucky stars that the cell was only an ordinary one in a district police station, and not within a big State prison from which there would have been no possible chance of escape.

It seemed ages to him before the frost had thawed sufficiently for him to risk gripping the stonework. At last he dared it and dropped down into the gloom outside.

'This way!' came the girl's voice from the night emptiness and by the cold she emanated Will guessed he was within speaking distance of her. He kept within range as she led the way swiftly through the quiet back streets of the city, only calling a halt when they were reasonably sure of immunity from pursuit.

'I hope you've worked this out properly,' Will said seriously. 'Don't forget I'm a fugitive on the run. I haven't even stood trial yet and if I'm recaptured things will be pretty hot for me.'

'If it comes to that, we're both fugitives,' she said — then as she sensed his surprise she continued: 'You said you were puzzled as to why I had returned to aid you. The truth is that I decided to find out if what you had said about human beings being unhurt by all forms of radio waves was correct. I found that it was; that you had killed my friends quite unintentionally. I saw that I'd wronged you, and that it is the gulf of sensory perception between us that led to my mistaken conclusions. So I called off the reprisal I'd started — that of having electrical machines, invisible to human beings, placed at different parts of London. They slowed down the molecular vibrations of the atmosphere and thereby produced arctic conditions. Had I gone to the limit and slowed the molecules down to zero, life itself would have ceased to exist.'

'So that's what you did! And in calling it off you made it look as though I'd been responsible for the whole thing. I was arrested because — '

'Yes, yes, I know why you were arrested. I saw the newspapers this morning and, realismg what had happened, I decided to get you out of jail — But I said I am a fugitive, too — and I am. The beings of this other plane cannot even now believe that your radio wave was not intended to harm them. I've tried to explain to them, but it's no use. Finally I destroyed the machines likely to produce arctic conditions and hurried to help you. But in so doing I've made it look as if I've forsaken my friends for you — their attacker. They're after me, just as the police are after you. And don't forget that in this other plane I am visible . . . '

The girl paused, then after a moment or two resumed: 'I don't see any signs of them at the moment. I told you I could adjust my vision to either plane, didn't I? I can see here, too, though it's dark to you.'

'But what's the answer to all this?' Will demanded desperately. 'We can't stand here theorising when we're both in danger. Where do we go? I can't go back to my shop because if I did that — '

'I know a place where we'll be reasonably safe. At any rate, you will, and I can look after myself. In my own plane the location is a pretty quiet spot. Follow me.'

Will did so, for an hour and more. They left the city behind and he found himself making his way across frozen ditches and iron-hard meadows, which had not yet thawed from the general relaxation of cold. At last he beheld a small wooden building looming up in the rising moonlight, set back on an elevated stretch of road.

'How about that?' the girl called out.

'Looks all right,' Will agreed. 'But to whom does it belong? We may be caught — '

'I've made sure of everything. It belongs to the Alvis Construction Company, but they went out of business a long time ago. It will probably be quite a while before anybody else takes over.'

'Nice work!' Will breathed. 'But look, two of us can't be in that place at the same time. You'd freeze me to death.'

'And if you put on too much heat you'd hurt me,' the girl pointed out. 'I can't stand large quantities of heat waves any more than you can stand scalding water. So I've worked out a compromise. I've taken a fur coat from a shop window for you to wear, and also a heater and some oil in a can. You can put on the fur coat and use the heater at half power. In that way I think we'll just about make it.'

'Then you're a lot more sanguine than I am,' Will sighed, starting to follow again. 'The way I see it, it seems we'll only sit

196

tight until we're eventually caught.'

'No we won't. I've got some ideas about that, too. I'll explain them later — Here we are!'

Obviously the girl had been here before for Will noticed that the door padlock was crumbled ash and that she walked straight in. He waited; then her voice came out of the intense gloom.

'Oh, I'm so sorry! I forgot that you can't see in the dark . . . Come in, and see if you can stand my presence. The oil lamp's on the table.'

Will fumbled around, hands and face pricking with cold. He found the lamp at last and the box of matches beside it. To his surprise the girl gave a cry of pain as the light came up.

'My own fault,' she said, after a moment or two. 'I ought to have shut my eyes for a while. I can only take light in easy doses . . . '

Will chafed his hands and looked about him. Big splashes of frost were on the bare wood walls and against the rough furniture where the girl was standing in a far corner. He moved to the door and shut it, then drew the battered old blind over the window. Apparently this place had once been a surveyor's hut. In various directions were rules, theodolites, and tape measures. In the corner opposite the girl was the oil stove she had brought, a can of paraffin oil, one or two pots and pans, a kettle, and tins of food.

'Nice going!' Will commented, flapping his arms vigorously.

'I had to carry them in blankets to save cracking them with cold. The blankets were in shreds when I got here. How will that fur coat do? I think I covered it up enough to save it.'

Will picked up the fur coat from the chair back and dragged it on thankfully. Then he turned the heat up half way and began to get a meal together. It was as he was in the midst of this that a thought struck him.

'Just how do you eat?' he asked, pondering.

'At present I'm limited to the food of my own plane. I'll get some later on. You eat yours whilst I set about telling you a few things.'

Will nodded and when he got around to pouring himself some tea the girl said: 'You got pretty close to working out the reverse system of your father's invention, didn't you? I went to your shop and found that the police had taken away your apparatus — but they'd left your notes behind. From them I could tell that — '

'I had it solved,' Will interrupted, his face grim. 'Solved, I tell you! Then the police had to blow in and gum up the works! It's the very devil!'

'There may be a way round that. This shed is directly under a group of high-tension wires. Probably, though, you didn't notice them in the dark. Suppose you had the necessary components and could clip cables to the high-tension wires, do you think there's be a chance of getting me back to normal?'

'A chance!' Will echoed. 'I know I could! But — there's a snag. The components I need are all at my shop and I just daren't return to get any — '

'No; but I can, and I will. I'll wrap them all up well so they won't get damaged. You see, Will, you've got to get me out of this before my erstwhile friends in this plane catch up on me.'

'Okay. That being so I'll write down a list of what I need and you'll have to memorise it . . . '

* * *

Existence for Will was a pretty nerve-racking business from that night onwards. Daylight revealed to him that the surveyor's hut was a good way from the beaten track, as unlikely a spot as any for the police to find him.

Vera returned at intervals, always with the cold air and frost, which presaged her arrival. Each time she returned with some new collection of vital components wrapped in fast rotting blanket, which looked as though it had been dipped in liquid air. Always she worked at night, and in different parts of the city certain radio dealers were becoming a nuisance in their demands that the police trace an unknown thief who was mysteriously robbing them.

Some of the materials Vera brought

from Will's own shop, necessary parts which only he could provide — and the more stuff she brought the harder Will worked, entirely from memory, the time he had spent poring over the original apparatus was now standing him in good stead.

'You realise, of course,' he said, when they were together on the third night, 'that when I switch this thing on two things can happen? If the police are busy with detectors — as they invariably are to trace illegal radio transmissions — they'll discover the origin of this instrument, and incidentally me. In your own plane your former friends are liable to get hurt yet again, but that is something I cannot avoid.'

'Yes, I've foreseen all that,' the girl responded, 'but as far as I'm concerned nothing matters. My former friends have seen fit to turn against me, so they must take the consequences. It's you I'm worrying about, Will. If the police should locate you before this job is finished we'll both be lost. I can never keep clear of my former friends long enough to rescue you for the second time. Besides, the police will see to it that there is no second time.'

'Yes, you're right enough there . . . ' Will considered for a moment and then shrugged. 'Well, we'll have to risk everything on one throw of the dice. No tests, no anything, in case we give things away. You game?'

'You bet I am!'

Will turned back to his work and thereafter toiled without a break for nearly three hours. At the end of it he was stiff, decidedly weary, but triumphant.

'Shan't be long now,' he said quickly, collecting together a length of double cable. 'I'm going to see what I can do to 'pirate' the high-tension wires.'

Once outside in the night he headed for the nearest pylon and then began the difficult climb up the braced steel bars to the summit. Once here he had to go to work with infinite care, protected by heavy rubber-leather gloves. First he reached out and clipped on one wire; then the other. When at last he got back to his apparatus he found everything was working perfectly.

'Something occurs to me,' came the girl's voice, after a moment. 'Isn't there a chance of the power station noting the extra load you're taking?'

'Every chance. I'm afraid, but it may take them quite a long time to trace it, and the first place they'll look will probably be in the city — not here. I'm not using up such a terrific lot of juice, anyway . . . ' Will hesitated, his hand on the switch control. 'Listen, Vera, in spite of what I said earlier I've got to make one small test in order to be sure. Without it I cannot be sure that you'll come through the experiment without harm.'

'Up to you. What do want me to do?'

'You'd better go outside if you will — to a distance of about half-a-mile. I'll give you five minutes.'

'All right — but the actual job will have to follow afterwards, no matter what, because we'll have given ourselves completely away.'

'I know. Just get going.'

Will waited impatiently after the girl had gone, his eye on his wristwatch. Immediately the five minutes were up he switched on the apparatus. His eyes brightened as he made a quick checkover. The power meters and other complicated devices would show him exactly what was happening, and as far as he could determine everything was in order. Smiling to himself he switched off and presently Vera returned.

'It works!' Will told her excitedly. 'Definitely it works! It's force of some kind, same as that which blasted you into that other plane — only it works in a different way now. As far as I can tell your bodily molecular structure, which was so upset by the original experiment, should now be restored to normal. I'm afraid it will hurt you but I'll stake everything I've got it will turn you into a visible human being in this plane.'

'Good! That's all we want to know — and I don't mind what risks we take because there's no turning back now. Let's get the job done.'

At that, Will threw the switch, directing the field towards the frosty area in the corner of the hut — then he turned with a puzzled frown as the smell of burning rubber floated to him and the whining of the dynamo suddenly ceased —

'The main cable!' he gasped in horror. 'You must have trodden on it, or something and it's rotted away!' He made a sudden dive. 'Yes, it's broken in two — Mind out! You may get hurt!'

Unwittingly he flung out his hand in a warning gesture and for a second contacted something yielding — but that something was as searing as the top of a white-hot stove. Anguish ripped at his finger-ends and brought tears into his eyes.

'Will, you touched me! Your hand — ' Vera's distraught voice came suddenly.

'Skip it!' Will panted. 'It's — it's frostbite, or something. Go outside again while I fix this.'

It was far more than frostbite, as Will soon found out. On his right hand, the first and second fingers were white to the knuckles, dead, seared with that inconceivable coldness. It hampered every move he made, made him fumble helplessly in his efforts to catch together the severed pieces of cable.

He worked as rapidly as he could, gritting his teeth against pain, but he was bitterly aware that he had lost fifteen precious minutes before he at last had the break repaired and the wire clumsily patched up with cylinders of rubber and insulating tape.

He got to his feet, gave the job a final once-over, and then moved towards the door to tell the girl to return. At the same moment, however, he heard her entry and fell back quickly. A second or two later her startled voice reached him.

'Will, they're coming! *They're coming!'*

'What! The police, you mean? But how have they — '

'No, no, the other beings! My enemies! I can see them. You must have killed off more of them and they know that where you are I will be also — Get that thing going before they find me, for God's sake! They'll turn heat-rays on me — They have done!' she finished, with a sudden shriek.

Will slammed the switch and the dynamo climbed steadily up into maximum revs — but above it he could hear something else. The sound of a car engine from somewhere quite near, and it was becoming louder.

'Will, hurry!' the girl cried desperately. 'The heat — !'

Her voice broke off and Will heard a thud. The bentwood chair went flying before an impact and frost cascaded along the floor. It was her fallen body: he knew that. He turned the projector downwards so that its power would still envelop her. Dead or alive, he had got to see just once what this mysterious girl looked like . . . Will's gaze rose suddenly from the floor to three grim faces in the open doorway of the hut — the faces of police officers. There was no mistaking them. At the moment they were holding back from the unbearable waves of cold beating around them.

'We've got you covered, Gregory,' one of them said. 'Switch off that cold-wave machine or take what's coming to you! You've got exactly ten seconds from — now.'

'Ten seconds are all I need,' Will retorted, glancing over his instruments.

'Wait and see for yourselves, then you can do whatever you want. You won't believe it, but there's a woman lying there on the floor — where that frost is. An invisible woman. She caused that cold spell which struck us. I had nothing to do with it. I'm bringing her back to visibility so she can answer to whatever charge there is — '

'Stop lying, Gregory! Our detectors show — '

'There!' Will shouted abruptly. 'Look! You can't gainsay the evidence of your own eyes!'

Will was trembling so much from the reaction of pain and excitement he could hardly stand but his urgent words had an effect on the police. The icy cold was commencing to relax. The three men in the doorway stood stupefied, staring blankly at something beginning to take outline on the floor amidst the energy field. A solitary hand all by itself became visible first; then the receding tide of invisibility revealed a bare and slender arm. Still further the invisibility dissolved and a head, neck and shoulders came into sight. Within perhaps fifty seconds the whole graceful body had come into view, face downwards and nude, since the other-world clothes had gone too.

'The Ice Maiden cometh,' Will whispered, then sprang forward and shut off the machine. Tugging off his fur coat he flung it over the girl, then he raised her gently and stared into her face. Somehow, it was vaguely as he had imagined it. Oval in shape, framed in black hair. The mouth was firm and sensitive, the brows arching and intelligent. He wondered what colour her eyes might be.

Anxiously he felt her pulse, then smiled in relief. It was beating strongly enough.

'All right,' the leading officer said, struggling out of his bewilderment. 'Get this woman round and let's hear what she has to say for herself.'

Will found himself elbowed out of the way and Vera was laid back on the floor whilst professional restoration was applied. At length the girl's eyes opened slowly — large brown ones — and she stared mystifiedly around her. Then at last she looked across to where Will was standing.

'Will . . . ' He could hardly hear her

voice. 'Will, you made it! I just remember them getting me when I collapsed! You — you brought me back!'

'Uh-huh,' Will acknowledged quietly, studying her.

'Yes, he brought you back,' the police officer-in-charge growled. 'And you're lucky that we happened to see it all take place otherwise we'd never have believed it. But you've certainly got a lot of explaining to do. Soon as you're all right we'll get moving.'

Will gave a grim smile. 'We can explain things okay — and open up a new field of scientific endeavour, maybe. As for me, the price will be two amputated fingers, I'm afraid.' He held up the dead-white members and sighed. 'Anyway, we'll get the scientists to trace Vera Morton's experience in full, then perhaps we'll get off with a year or two.'

'Or else — life,' Vera murmured, and buttoned the fur coat tightly about her.

CLIMATE INCORPORATED
THE FIVE MATCHBOXES
EXCEPT FOR ONE THING
BLACK MARIA, M.A.
ONE STEP TOO FAR
THE THIRTY-FIRST OF JUNE
THE FROZEN LIMIT
ONE REMAINED SEATED
THE MURDERED SCHOOLGIRL
SECRET OF THE RING
OTHER EYES WATCHING
I SPY . . .
FOOL'S PARADISE
DON'T TOUCH ME
THE FOURTH DOOR
THE SPIKED BOY
THE SLITHERERS
MAN OF TWO WORLDS
THE ATLANTIC TUNNEL
THE EMPTY COFFINS
LIQUID DEATH
PATTERN OF MURDER
NEBULA
THE LIE DESTROYER
PRISONER OF TIME

MIRACLE MAN
THE MULTI-MAN
THE RED INSECTS
THE GOLD OF AKADA
RETURN TO AKADA
GLIMPSE
ENDLESS DAY
THE G-BOMB
A THING OF THE PAST
THE BLACK TERROR
THE SILENT WORLD
DEATH ASKS THE QUESTION
A CASE FOR BRUTUS LLOYD
LONELY ROAD MURDER
THE HAUNTED GALLERY
SPIDER MORGAN'S SECRET

We do hope that you have enjoyed reading this large print book.

Did you know that all of our titles are available for purchase?

We publish a wide range of high quality large print books including:
Romances, Mysteries, Classics
General Fiction
Non Fiction and Westerns

Special interest titles available in large print are:
The Little Oxford Dictionary
Music Book, Song Book
Hymn Book, Service Book

Also available from us courtesy of Oxford University Press:
Young Readers' Dictionary
(large print edition)
Young Readers' Thesaurus
(large print edition)

For further information or a free brochure, please contact us at:
Ulverscroft Large Print Books Ltd.,
The Green, Bradgate Road, Anstey,
Leicester, LE7 7FU, England.
Tel: (00 44) **0116 236 4325**
Fax: (00 44) **0116 234 0205**

Other titles in the
Linford Mystery Library:

THE DEVIL'S DOZEN

Nigel Vane

In the underworld of London, the 'Stranger' controlled the 'Devil's Dozen', a gang noted for the daring and murderous nature of their crimes. However, the Stranger intended to betray his gang members to the police and leave himself with all the proceeds of their crimes. Then one gang member found out the Stranger's plan and his identity — and was quickly silenced. Private investigator Philip Quest was determined to unmask the Stranger. Would he live long enough to do it?

THEY WALK IN DARKNESS

Gerald Verner

Horrifying events in the village of Fendyke St. Mary left lambs with their throats cut. This was followed by the disappearance and murder of six young children — all with their throats cut. Then the bodies of two men and two women were found in Witch's House, a derelict cottage — all poisoned. Yet strangely, the murder had occurred whilst the cottage was surrounded by snow; and after locking the door, the murderer had escaped leaving no tracks . . .

FANATICS

Steve Hayes & David Whitehead

Special Agent Gus Novacek has orders from the President to stop Koji Shaguma's sinister Armageddon cult before it destroys the world. But it seems that Gus is always one step behind the murderous fanatics, as Armageddon strikes in Tokyo, Paris, London and finally New York. Then, a hijacked plane, bound for Algiers and rapidly losing fuel, is about to crash in the Atlantic with everyone on board . . . unless Gus can find a way to avert total disaster.

I SHALL AVENGE!

John Robb

When Kriso Tovak joins the Foreign Legion, he believes his beloved wife to be dead. However, discovering that she's still alive, Tovak deserts to join his wife in Prague. But he's captured, court-martialled and executed, which sparks a series of ghastly events in the Legion base at Dini Sadazi. And at the heart of it all is Annice Tovak, who takes terrible vengeance for the death of her husband . . .